Cimarron Sunrise

A Novel by ...

BRENDA TURNER

Brenda Turner

Cimarron Sunrise
ISBN: 978-0-88144-265-6
Copyright © 2010 by Brenda Turner

Published by
Yorkshire Publishing
9731 East 54th Street
Tulsa, OK 74146
www.yorkshirepublishing.com

Lovingly dedicated to my parents who allowed a little girl to dream large. As always, my love to Curtis, Summer, Jacqueline, Conner, and Venda. Thank you for your enthusiastic support of my writing.

Biscuits and Bushwhackers

Steam from the warm kitchen fogged the windowpane. Maddy was sitting with her back to the coal-burning stove, getting toasty warm before the walk to school. Selecting one of Granny's melt-in-your-mouth biscuits from the white platter on the table, she carefully chewed it, fanning her open mouth in a very unladylike way. Ma gave her a glancing frown. Maddy knew better than to eat biscuits straight from the oven, but it was always hard to resist Granny's delicious food. She was reaching for another biscuit when Grandpa stormed through the back door, letting it slam behind him.

"I don't know what this world is coming to!" he exclaimed.

Maddy dropped her biscuit, shocked by Grandpa's behavior.

"John!" warned Granny. "The children are listening."

Grandpa surveyed the warm kitchen, taking in the surprised faces of his family. He gave his head a little shake. "I'm sorry," he said "I'm just frustrated. When I went into town early this morning to get a paper, I heard that a gang of bushwhackers broke out from the Jackson County Jail last night. Luckily, the marshal isn't hurt too bad. There was a scuffle and they took off with his pistol and rifles." He set the newspaper on the worn kitchen table. "I hope they aren't holed up in town! I hate knowing they're out there somewhere, looking for their next victim."

Maddy couldn't hold in her question any longer, "Grandpa, what's a bushwhacker?" She sheepishly tossed the dropped biscuit into the scrap pail while waiting for his answer.

"Bushwhackers are bad men, Maddy. They're men who rob good folks while they're out traveling. Usually they rob people who they think are carrying money or who are easy targets for stealing their horses."

Granny gave a nod to Grandpa. "Why don't we change the subject, John, before your biscuits get cold?"

Grandpa understood. He unfolded the newspaper. "Let's see what's going on in Independence, Missouri, these days," he said as he began scanning the articles. "Hmmm, listen to this. President Harrison has signed an order that the Unassigned Lands in Indian Territory be opened for settlement." Grandpa paused, reading further. "Goodness, this is a plumb fool notion! The government is going to have a land run—a race—to decide who will get the land that's being opened! It sounds as if anyone who can make it to a claim of land can take it, all 160 acres. Why, that's a quarter of a square mile!"

"The land is really free, John?" asked Ma. Even though Ma had turned back to stir the gravy, Maddy could tell she was listening closely to the article in the Kansas City Star by the tilt of her head and the way the stirring spoon slowed in the cast iron pan.

"From what I can tell it's free," replied Grandpa. "The land run is set for April 22nd. That's just next month. I don't know how the government would think people could get their things ready for such a move in that short of a time."

Grandpa finished reading the article aloud while Maddy ate another, cooler biscuit. She wondered why Ma appeared to be so interested in the story about folks running in a horse race. Racing with hundreds of other people didn't sound like fun to Maddy. To her it sounded like a dirty, ugly mess.

"Ready to go, Maddy?" asked Nick, interrupting her thoughts, as he slung his leather book bag over his shoulder.

Maddy scraped her chair back. "Give me a minute," she replied as she dashed up the narrow stairs off the kitchen to snatch her blue calico bonnet and McGuffey reader from her room. Buttoning their coats as they stood at the back door, the pair left for school, waving farewell to Ma, Granny, and Grandpa.

"Be good today, you two," Ma called after them.

Nick and Maddy sauntered the eight blocks down the street to the schoolhouse. Drifts of snow slanted along the sides. Luckily, there weren't many wagons out, so they could walk down the center of the road and keep their boots free of snow.

"Nick, did you understand what Grandpa was reading about in the newspaper?" Maddy asked.

"From what I could tell, it was an article about a land run. The federal government is going to open up the Indian Territory for settlement. Anyone who wants to have some of the free land can get on the starting line, and then when the cavalry shoots the gun to start the race, people can race and claim the free land."

"Didn't you think Ma seemed specially interested in what Grandpa was reading? Why would she even ask about something like going off to get free land? Doesn't she like living with Grandpa and Granny?"

"It's always bothered Ma that we have to live with Pa's folks instead of being on our own. But after Pa died from the accident, she really didn't have a way to support us. That's why we had to move here to live with Granny and Grandpa."

"But I like it here!" Maddy exclaimed. She didn't see what the big deal was with them living with Granny and Grandpa. Her grandparents had made it very clear that they enjoyed having them living at the house. She couldn't understand why anyone would find excitement in a big old dirty race with the prize being a piece of land. She liked living with Granny and Grandpa.

At Granny and Grandpa's house she had her own pretty upstairs bedroom, decorated special for her. Granny had picked out wallpaper with pink roses all over it and had made a quilt to match when they moved in. She even had a hooked rug to cover the floor planks. None of her friends had such a pretty room. In fact, most of her friends had to share rooms with their other family members. If what she'd heard Grandpa read from the paper was true, some people who got land in Indian Territory would be building houses out of sod and dirt. Nasty! Maddy definitely didn't want to be tucked into bed at night next to walls filled with dirt and bugs! She wouldn't know what to do if a worm were peeking at her in the morning when she woke up.

"But what do *you* think, Nick, about what Grandpa was reading in the newspaper?" she asked.

Nick flashed his big grin, and his brown eyes sparkled, "Whoa, Maddy! That would be the most amazing thing in the world, to be in a horse race where the prize is to pick your piece of land to live in and claim forever! I wish I was old enough to go get a piece of land; I'd do it for us!"

"Why would you want to leave Granny and Grandpa's house?" asked Maddy. Nick glanced down at his little sister. It surprised him sometimes to see how she was starting to grow up. At nine years old, she was almost as high as his shoulder now. Her brown eyes were fringed with thick black lashes, and her smile could light up any room. She'd grow up to be as pretty as Ma, he guessed. He hoped that he would grow to be as strong as Pa had been.

"Maddy, I really don't think you have anything to worry about," Nick assured her. "Ma would never pack up a wagon and drive us three hundred miles to make a claim of land. I wish I could do it, but I know she wouldn't let me leave. Anyway, according to the article, I'm not legally old enough to hold a claim of land. And that's not even considering how dangerous the trip to the starting line would be."

Maddy knew Nick felt he should be the man of the house since Pa had died. Almost fifteen, he sometimes wondered if he should still be going to school or working with Grandpa in his building business. But Ma kept insisting that he get his schooling for as long as possible. There had even been some discussion that Nick might someday go to Liberty College.

"I guess I'll just have to hope that I have an opportunity to make another land run someday," he said.

Maddy and Nick were approaching the schoolyard. Before joining the other children, Nick stopped and turned to look Maddy squarely in the eye. "Listen, Maddy, don't talk about any of this around your little friends. Even though nothing will come of it, I know Ma wouldn't appreciate other people knowing she'd even been discussing the land run with Grandpa."

Maddy nodded, her straw-colored braids bobbing. She did not want her friends to think any less of Ma. She'd just stay quiet about the whole idea. After all, there was no way Ma would do something as wild as taking off to go on a land run!

CHAPTER 2

Unwelcome Surprise

That morning wore on endlessly at the one-room schoolhouse. Miss Busby was stricter than ever, demanding perfection in the recitations. Maddy had practiced at her desk for almost an hour with the piece that

Miss Busby wanted her to recite, but it was hard to concentrate while worrying about what Ma was thinking about that land run. She could feel a knot starting to twist in her stomach. Besides, she didn't like having to get up in front of Miss Busby and the class and say the pieces from memory. She always worried that she'd freeze up and forget what she was supposed to say and make a fool of herself.

"Fourth grade, come to the front for recitations," Miss Busby called. She had a slicked-back bun and plain calico print dress brushing the tops of her worn but polished boots. Maddy sometimes wondered if Miss Busby would just teach forever. She knew it wasn't nice, but she called Miss Busby an "old maid" behind her back. With her pinched mouth, drab clothes, and sour personality, even a backwoods farmer wouldn't want to marry her! At least that was what Nick said. Maddy was so engrossed in her thoughts about Miss Busby and her lack of a beau that she didn't realize she'd been called on.

"Maddy, I called on you to come forward," said Miss Busby sharply. "Please do so at this time."

Miss Busby eyed Maddy sternly as she stepped onto the platform where the teacher's desk was centered. She turned to face Miss Busby, who was standing in the center aisle next to the bench holding the other fourth graders. Maddy's best friend, Clara, was smiling up at her, but Miss Busby's face was grim.

"Four score and seven years ago our fathers brought forth, upon this continent, a new nation, conceived in liberty, and dedicated to the proposition that all men are created equal," Maddy began. "Now we are engaged in a great civil war, testing whether that nation, or any nation—" Since February was the month of both President Lincoln's and President Washington's birthdays, Miss Busby had assigned speeches to be memorized from those two presidents. The students had been working on them all month. Now during March, they were taking turns reciting.

Maddy formed the words carefully, and as she spoke, she thought about the Civil War that had ended over twenty years ago. That seemed like ancient history, but Ma's daddy and grandfather had fought for the North.

With her mind on the war and the freedoms that it represented, she felt her voice grow stronger. President Lincoln was a good man, and he had wanted all men to be equal.

"You did a fine job, Maddy," said Miss Busby as Maddy concluded. "You portrayed good emotion as you recited. You may be seated at the bench. Clara, now it is time for you to recite."

Maddy was happy to be finished so she could listen to the others. She was even happier when she was allowed to return to her desk. She was more than ready to do her math ciphering on her gray slate and be out of the limelight.

Maddy was generally quiet in her activities. She enjoyed spending time with her friends. She loved to have fun and sometimes took part in Nick's tricks and games, but Nick was different. He was always loud and drew attention to himself, trying to be the best at everything so he could get the cheers (and sometimes jeers) during games at recess.

Finally three o'clock rolled around, and Miss Busby dismissed the students. Maddy grabbed her blue calico bonnet and empty lunch bucket from the cloakroom and dashed outside to wait for Nick, who was loitering in the schoolyard. He joined Maddy for the walk home. "Ole Buzzard was on a tear today, wasn't she?" he asked Maddy with a smile.

Maddy smiled at her brother. He wasn't supposed to call their teacher by that nickname, but he and the other big boys got away with it. Privately, Maddy thought the name fit, but she was too scared to ever say it out loud. "She was testy, that's for sure," replied Maddy. "I was glad to finish up with my recitation of the Gettysburg Address so I could get back to work on ciphering at my desk.

"Nick, have you thought anymore about that land run Grandpa was reading about this morning?"

Nick glanced down at Maddy. "I did think about it some when I was s'posed to be reading," Nick admitted. "I think it would be the grandest thing in the world to do something like that. Can you imagine, free land? Ma would love to have land of our own."

"But we live with Granny and Grandpa! They seem to like the fact that we live with them."

"Oh, *they* do like having us, mind you. But you know our Ma, and she likes to be independent, not relying on anyone. I know it bothers her to have to live with Pa's folks, even though I know that we are welcome."

"Well, I'm not going to bring it up. Surely Ma has already forgotten all about it."

Going up the back steps, Nick and Maddy could smell apple pie baking, the scent of cinnamon wafting sweetly in the air. Opening the back door, they discovered that Granny was nowhere to be found, but Ma was pacing back and forth in front of the hot oven. "Welcome home, children," she said distractedly as she turned to pull out the pie. Nick and Maddy shared a glance as they dropped their book bags on the sturdy bench by the back door.

"The pie smells delicious, Ma," said Maddy as she wrapped her arms around Ma's slender waist for a hug.

"Do I have to wait until supper to have a piece?" Nick chimed in.

Ma ignored Nick's question. "Sit down, children; we need to talk," she said. She opened the oven door and, using towels to protect her hands, pulled the pie out of the oven. She carefully set the pie on a clean towel on the windowsill to cool then joined Nick and Maddy at the table. Maddy looked from Ma's face to Nick's. Nick was studying Ma's expression intently, trying to read her expression.

After a few moments of silence, he ventured, "Ma—are you thinking about what I think you're thinking about?"

"That's a silly sentence, Nick. Miss Busby wouldn't be pleased with your grammar! Whatever are you talking about?"

"You know, from this morning, the article about the land run?"

Ma gave a sigh, dropped her head into her hands, then gave a nod.

Maddy felt her heart drop. She couldn't believe Ma admitted that she was even thinking about the land run. This couldn't be happening to her! She did not want to go live in Indian Territory. Maddy looked over at Nick. He had a goofy grin plastered across his face. She could tell that he would be no help convincing Ma that this was a bad idea.

Ma raised her head and looked at both children. "I know you probably think I'm crazy, but I know we can do this. We can make this run, and I can own a piece of land outright and build a future for the two of you."

Nick's face lit up. He was proud of his ma. None of his friends' mothers had the courage to do something like this!

"We're going to have to work fast to pull this off, though," Ma continued. "To get supplies ready, a wagon together, and make the trip to the starting line, we're going to have to start working on our preparations tomorrow."

Grandpa and Granny entered the warm kitchen. Granny promptly went over to scoop Maddy into her arms and hold her on the chair. Ma said that Maddy was too big to be held like that, but Maddy didn't think so. Granny always made her feel loved, and when Maddy was with her and Grandpa, she always felt safe.

"You're really going to do this, Ellen?" asked Grandpa. "I worry about you and the children down there with the Indians so near."

"This land isn't assigned to a tribe. We'll be just fine," said Ma.

Granny chimed in, "Well, what about bushwhackers? That gang just got out of jail and goodness knows a woman and two children would be an easy target." Maddy's eyes grew even rounder as she considered traveling for days all alone, with no man with them for protection.

"Jeanette!"

Maddy's head snapped up. She had never heard Ma use such a frightening tone with Granny.

"That's enough. We'll be safe, and there's no reason to alarm Maddy." Ma looked at Maddy and gave her a warm smile. "Darlin', there will be nothing to fear. We can do this! And once we're settled, Granny and Grandpa will take a stagecoach or train and come visit us."

Maddy looked from Ma to Granny. Granny's lips were set in a firm white line and Maddy could tell she was displeased. Even though her long legs were dragging the floor, Maddy snuggled in closer to her grandmother, as if she could somehow give Maddy protection from the cold outside the house and the chilly fear in her heart.

Granny leaned down and whispered ever-so-softly in her ear, "You can stay with me if you want."

Maddy glanced up, and her brown eyes locked with Granny's piercing blue gaze. Granny gave an imperceptible nod, and Maddy glanced down at her scuffed boots, ashamed at how her heart had leapt to think of getting to stay with Granny and Grandpa. Ma would be heartsick if she knew that Maddy would rather wave goodbye to her and Nick than join them.

"That's enough talk for now," Ma said. "We'll sit down at the kitchen table after supper and come up with our plan. You will help us, won't you John?" This time, Maddy could hear the tremors in Ma's voice. She looked over at her strong grandfather, whose shoulders were just beginning to hunch over. His hair had turned silver, but he could still split wood and swing a hammer just as quickly as the young men who worked for his building company. But for the first time, Maddy could see a weariness in Grandpa's body that she hadn't seen before. He looked worn out.

John looked at his wife holding their only granddaughter. Then he looked over at Ma and Nick with their glowing faces. "Yes," he agreed, a note of sadness in his voice. "I'll help you, if you're bound and determined to do this thing. Jeanette and I would rather you stayed here with us, but I can understand your need to build a future for your young'uns. And, with free land being offered, you'll never have another opportunity like this one.

"It is going to take time to get a wagon ready, and it is pert near 250 miles to where you'll line up for the race. Considering that a covered wagon is only going to get about fifteen miles a day on the trail, not counting how slow it will be in poor weather, we should have started getting you ready last month."

Maddy began ciphering in her head: 250 miles at 15 miles a day. It would take close to twenty days to get there. Three weeks of traveling in a covered wagon with bugs and wild animals for company. No fresh apple pie hot from the oven or Granny's lap to hold her when she needed it. She pictured her pretty room upstairs and shivered at the thought of bugs crawling around in those pink roses. She dreaded her future.

"We'll start building tomorrow," Grandpa continued. "Nick is going to have to stay home from school to help. Maddy can still go. It'll be hard to know how long until they start building schools down in the Territory, so she needs to get as much schooling as possible. From my calculations, I'd say you three need to be on the trail as soon as possible to allow for any bad weather that may crop up."

Nick let out a whoop. No more school for him, and he was glad. "What do we need to get, Grandpa, for the wagon?"

Grandpa reached for a piece of brown paper and his carpenter's pencil. "Let's sit down here and start figuring it out, son."

As Maddy looked back and forth between the dearest adults in her life, she realized that this was not just a notion. Ma really did plan to take them to live near the Indians. And Grandpa was going to help them get on the road!

Sevens

Maddy was scowling as she left the house the following morning. At breakfast, Nick had been more than happy to rub it in that he was staying home to work on their trip. As Maddy left the yard, she gave Nick a quick wave, but he was so intent on listening to what Grandpa was telling him that he didn't even see her. Now his job was to help Grandpa build the wagon and get the supplies gathered for their move.

Maddy dreaded walking by herself to school in the chilly morning. Walking with Nick always made the trip to school seem like an adventure, but when she was alone, her thoughts could ramble like a lost calf. She carefully sidestepped the patches of ice that had refrozen during the night, alone with her worries about Ma's plans to make the land run.

Deep in thought, Maddy didn't even hear the familiar chime of the schoolhouse bell. Miss Busby had stepped out onto the top step of the schoolhouse porch to greet her scholars. Students were running as quickly as possible to line up for the march into the building.

"Maddy, hurry up, Miss Busby'll have your hide!" Clara called breathlessly. Clara was Maddy's dearest friend on earth. Looking at her smiling blue eyes, Maddy felt her own chocolate ones well with tears. She'd probably never see Clara again once they moved to

Indian Territory. Maddy quickly dropped her head to hide the tears.

"Maddy, you look like you're about to cry. Where's Nick?"

Maddy just shook her head. She feared that if she opened her mouth she'd start crying like a baby. Miss Busby was scowling down on them in the back of the girls' line. Maddy nodded towards Miss Busby and the girls fell into line without any further discussion. Once the last child had gotten in line, Miss Busby turned on her heel sharply to lead everyone into the schoolhouse. Nick always joked that she would have made a good soldier with the way she walked and carried herself. Maddy set her lunch bucket on the cabinet in the cloakroom and hung her bonnet and overcoat on a peg.

"Maddy," whispered Clara again, "What is going on?"

Maddy gave a shrug. "Nothing," she whispered back. "I'm fine."

The morning dragged on endlessly. Maddy stumbled over her lessons. She did so poorly with her ciphering that even Miss Busby took note. "Feeling ill today, Maddy?" she frowned. "Is Nicholas home sick?"

"No, ma'am. I mean, I'm all right. Nick is home helping my Grandpa."

"Your mother shouldn't allow Nicholas to miss his schooling. It isn't becoming for a young man living in the city not to have his education. And if he's serious about Liberty College, he has to pass this school with honors."

"Yes, ma'am," replied Maddy, wondering what good an education would do Nick in the midst of Indian Territory. Of course, Miss Busby had no way of knowing that two of her students would soon be leaving.

The morning lessons finally came to an end. Miss Busby went up on the platform and announced, "Scholars, it is time for your dinner. You may get your things and eat or run on home."

When the weather was nice, Nick and Maddy often went back home for lunch. Granny and Ma would have a hot meal waiting for them, and they enjoyed the break from the classroom. But in wintertime, they stayed and took their dinner at school, eating from large lunch buckets packed with biscuits, strips of Grandpa's smoked ham, and Granny's delicious apple butter. The cold lunches weren't ever as good as what they got at home, but Maddy looked forward to having time to visit with Clara since Clara always ate her lunch at the schoolhouse.

The two girls gathered near the warm stove to eat and play a game of Buzz. This was Maddy's favorite game, but today she had trouble focusing.

"Eighteen," she said.

"You're out!" cried Clara. "Let's play for sevens."

The girls began to play, each counting up by one and calling, "Buzz!" when they stopped on a multiple of seven. Maddy missed again, saying "twenty-eight" instead of "buzz."

"Maddy, spill the beans," said Clara. "Sevens are usually your favorite, and you're missing them left and right! What's the problem? Whatever it is can't be too bad, or your ma wouldn't have let you come to school by yourself."

Maddy looked into her friend's concerned face and couldn't hold in her feelings any longer. "Ma's going to make a claim in the land run," she blurted. "We're all moving to Indian Territory for the free land. We'll leave for the starting line as soon as Grandpa and Nick can get the wagon ready to travel."

"What do you mean, land run? Whatever are you talking about?"

"It was in yesterday's *Kansas City Star*— the ad for free land. Grandpa started reading about it at breakfast like he always does with any news that catches his interest. But Ma perked up when she heard that settlers would get a free quarter section of land. She and Grandpa must have done some investigating of how it all worked yesterday while we were at school."

Clara seemed stunned. "You mean you and your ma and Nick and your grandparents are going to make this land run? And what exactly is a land run again?"

"From what I can tell, a land run is just a big race. There'll be people lined up to race as fast as they can, only the prize won't be a blue ribbon; it'll be 160 acres of free land, a quarter of a square mile. Granny and Grandpa aren't coming with us. It's just Ma and me and Nick. Women without a husband can stake and hold down a claim. Ma wants to make sure Nick and I have land of our own."

Once Clara got over her initial astonishment, she cried, "But Maddy, will you be safe? Will I ever see you again?"

Maddy's eyes welled up with tears again. "I don't know, Clara. Granny said I could stay and live with her and Grandpa, but I think I'd just die if I never got to be with Nick and Ma again." Her lip trembled. "I'm just so scared. I don't know if I'm more scared about living in Indian Territory or the trip to get to the starting line. Did your pa hear about the bushwhackers that escaped from the jail?" Her voice dropped to a ragged whisper. "What if they're out there somewhere, waiting to rob us?"

Clara could only pat Maddy on the shoulder, unsure of how to console her best friend.

CHAPTER 4

Memories

The afternoon had seemed endless, but finally Miss Busby rang the bell, signaling the end of the school day. As Maddy neared her grandparents' house after the lonely walk home, she was surprised to see

Grandpa's wagon fitted with eight arches of bent hickory bows stretched across the wagon bed. The arches made the ten-by-four-foot wagon look tall. Seeing the wagon made the journey all too real.

Nick was methodically hammering long nails into the side panels. "Maddy!" he called cheerfully. "How was school?"

"Miserable," she replied. "Miss Busby was mad at me for not doing my ciphering well. And Clara is heartbroken about this wild idea." She looked up at her brother. "Do we really have to do this, Nick?"

Nick stopped hammering and looked down into his sister's face. Her freckles had faded in the winter months but he could still see a few across her nose. The corners of her mouth were tilted down and he could read the anguish in her eyes.

"Maddy," he said kindly, "you've got to see this as an opportunity that will never come again. No other territory has done this before, offering prime land for free to anyone who is willing to run hard and take what's there."

"But why does Ma want to leave here?" Maddy asked. "I just don't understand. I love living here with Granny and Grandpa."

"Ma wants us to have a future that's all our own. And you know Ma's got an independent streak a mile long! She wants this for herself as much as for us."

Maddy absorbed this last piece of information. All she could remember was Ma doing things for her and Nick and Pa while Pa was still alive. It was hard to imagine Ma wanting to take on this man's race. She'd never seen her ma really do anything outside of working in the home and helping care for the chickens and work some in their household vegetable garden.

Nick observed Maddy's puzzled expression. "You don't remember, do you, Maddy?"

"Remember what?"

At Maddy's look of puzzlement, Nick laid down his hammer and hopped off the wagon. "You don't remember Ma in those early days, do you?

"Before you were born, I can remember waking up to the sounds of gunshots and hearing her and Pa laughing out back of the barn. I'd open the door of the house and step outside. Pa'd see me and say, 'Come watch your Ma—she's the best shot for miles around.' Ma'd flash me one of her big smiles and then proceed to knock can after can off the fence post. When she hit the last one, she'd say, 'Now that's the way to get 'er done, boys!' She'd give me a big wink and then go into the house and fix our breakfast."

"Then Pa had the accident with the pitch-fork and got the infection; he just got sicker and sicker and was unable to get around. When he became bedfast, he seemed to give up his will to live. You were so young back then, you probably don't remember much about it."

"I remember him a little," Maddy said. "One time I went to the side of the bed and talked to him about the newest litter of kittens. Then one day I brought one to show him. He smiled and petted it, but that seemed to take all of his energy. It kind of seems like he just gradually melted away in that bed, getting weaker and weaker. Other than talking to him that one time about the kittens, I really don't have memories of him."

"Well, Ma was so worn out keeping up with our place and trying to nurse him back to health, it was like she just gave up that other adventurous part of herself. I never saw her shoot a gun again, and once Pa died and we had to sell our farm and move in with Granny and Grandpa, I didn't see her smile like that anymore. It's almost like when Pa died, that part of her died right along with him."

Maddy tried to picture Ma laughing and shooting targets with deadeye aim. The image didn't match the Ma she knew, who kept her hair in a neat bun and wore her sprigged calico dresses primly buttoned, with a starched white apron snugly tied around her waist. Nick had to be pulling her leg. "I don't believe you—all that about Ma shooting targets. That's not the Ma I know."

"Then ask her, Maddy. Let Ma tell you what's in her heart." Nick resumed hammering with a ferocity that surprised her. As she walked inside, her stomach felt all hollow. She felt completely out of control, as if her life was no longer in her hands.

"Welcome home, Maddy!" Granny called as Maddy stepped into the kitchen with her shoulders slumped. "How was school today?"

"Fine," replied Maddy tonelessly. She said nothing else as she unbuttoned the wool cloak and hung it on the oak peg by the door. "Where's Ma?"

Granny looked at Maddy sharply, as if she was trying to discern her thoughts. "She's out in the barn, sugar, with your Grandpa. They're looking for supplies to build boxes for your wagon." Granny noted the thin set of Maddy's lips. She turned to face Maddy head on. "Remember, Maddy, you can stay with me. You don't have to make this horrible move to Indian Territory."

Maddy knew she was being rude, but she had to get some answers. She glanced back at Granny as she grabbed her cloak again, flinging it around her shoulders before making the walk to the barn.

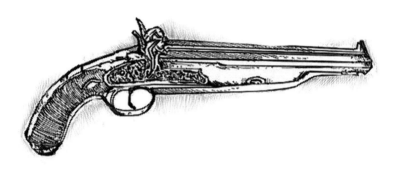

C H A P T E R   5

An Unlikely Friendship

Ma and Grandpa looked up when Maddy entered the barn. Grandpa took one look at the storm cloud brewing on Maddy's brow, turned to Ma and said, "I think Granny needs me to help her up at the house." He left the barn, and Maddy and Ma were alone. Ma took in Maddy's expression, the tight set of her lips, and simply reached out her arms.

As Ma held her, Maddy felt the hot tears begin to flow. She'd lost so much: Pa, their farm . . . and now it seemed they were going to lose Granny and Grandpa. Even worse than that, she felt like she'd somehow lost Ma. This woman who was willing to race in a land run to claim property among Indians just wasn't the Ma she knew.

"Maddy." Ma's voice was quiet as Maddy's tears began to subside. "Life has been hard for us, but that is going to change. We are going to take advantage of this opportunity. It's almost unbelievable that someone would just hand over free land.

"I know it's hard for you to imagine it now, but we're going to travel to Indian Territory, and when the cavalry blows their horns at high noon on April 22, we are going to get a piece of land that will be for the three of us."

"But Ma, I'm scared. We may get hurt or even die!" Maddy cried louder. "Who's going to protect us?"

Ma leaned back and tipped up Maddy's chin. "Look at me, Maddy. *I'm* going to protect us. There's a little-known fact about me that you don't know." Ma looked down at Maddy's wet face. She rubbed her heaving shoulders, "What you don't realize is that I was just about the fastest gun in Clay County."

Seeing Maddy's confusion, Ma smiled gently and said, "I think you'd better have a seat." She gestured to the hay bales that were stacked near the horse stalls. Ma spread a horse blanket on a bale of hay for Maddy and sat down across from her. The horses whickered softly in the background.

Ma bowed her head, looking at her hands. Maddy waited quietly. She was confused by what Ma had said and didn't know what to think. Ma raised her head. "I know it's strange for you to think about sometimes, but I was once a young girl, just like you." Ma smiled. "You never got to meet my parents. They died from influenza when I was only fifteen, but they would have loved to know you and Nick.

We had a farm outside of Kearney, and your other grandpa was a farmer. He raised hemp and was able to make a good living for all of us."

"Hemp? What's that?"

"My goodness, you are a city girl, aren't you? Hemp is a plant that is useful for many things. It was once used as money in our colonies, and our own Declaration of Independence and Constitution were drafted on hemp paper. Hemp seeds are very nutritious. I'd usually have a handful in my pockets just out of habit when I was your age. They can be eaten whole or ground into flour for baking. There are still hemp farmers today, but its uses are dwindling since more ships are being powered by steam and the hemp isn't as needed for cordage," Ma saw the confused look on Maddy's face. "Cordage is rope for ships, honey."

Maddy nodded.

"Anyway, I grew up much like you. Had to do chores, go to school. But unlike you, we lived out in the country, whereas you've grown accustomed to living in the city.

"I had only one sister. She was older and tended the house with my ma, so I was at loose ends a lot around the farm. Our neighbors to the east were a nice family, the Samuels. Their pa was a doctor in town. They had a few kids, so I'd often go over to their place to hang around since it was so boring at our house. We'd play games in the Samuels' backfield, sometimes kickball, sometimes have races.

"One of their sons was named Jesse. At times he'd clear all of us out of the way and set up cans along the back pasture fence. He loved showing off to us how well he could shoot a pistol. He never missed a can; sometimes he'd even play like his eyes were shut and still hit every single one of them. He was an amazing marksman, and I became fascinated by how he could shoot that pistol. No matter how far away the target, or what direction it would move, he could always hit it with deadeye aim.

"Well, back then I was as persistent as you are. I kept pestering him about wanting to shoot until he finally gave in and began teaching me how to use a pistol. I'd hurry home from school every day, and if I finished my chores really fast, I'd have time to run over to their place and practice shooting. There was no way my ma would have let me go if she'd known what we were up to! We'd go out behind the barn, and he'd set up targets along a back fence. We'd practice until time for me to go home for supper. He was patient with me, and by the time I was ten years old I was just as good a shot as he."

"You could shoot like that when you were practically my age?" asked Maddy in amazement. She'd never been allowed to handle guns, much less shoot one!

Ma smiled to herself. She was so intent on remembering her past that she hardly noticed Maddy. "Jesse took off from home when he was sixteen, but I never forgot his kindness to me nor the skills he taught me with a gun. Because of him, I'm not afraid to take on this challenge. You don't have to worry about being safe. Grandpa's getting our wagon outfitted the best possible way. I can protect us, and I'm going to start working with Nick on using the pistol as well. We can do this, Maddy, I know we can."

"But Ma, that was a long time ago! Can you still shoot? What if someone tries to rob us? Granny said that there might be bushwhackers out on the roadways, not to mention the Indians!"

"Maddy," said Ma, her voice lower, "I don't like to advertise this. In fact your Granny and Grandpa don't know it, and I think it would scare them if they did know. But I want *you* to know. Maybe it will help you understand that I can take care of us. Dr. Samuel was Jesse's stepfather. His real father, who died when Jesse was three years old, was Robert James. I learned how to shoot with the best...with Jesse James."

Maddy exhaled a long breath, almost as if she'd been holding her breath the entire time Ma had been speaking. "Jesse James? But, Ma, he was a real bad man!"

"I know, sugar. He did do some bad things, and I don't know what happened to him that caused him to get so off track. His pa was a minister and started Liberty College up in Clay County, where we'd talked about maybe sending Nick someday before your father died. And his stepfather, Dr. Samuels, was a kind man.

"Regardless of where Jesse ended up, he didn't start out trying to be bad. He was a wonderful brother to his sisters and brothers, and he was always kind and patient with me. I choose to remember young Jesse when I hear his name being bandied about."

Maddy's heart rose within her. She felt like she knew her Ma a little better now. Goodness, Ma'd been a friend to Jesse James! Maybe Ma *could* take care of her and Nick after all.

She looked up at Ma. "I can't believe you're such a good shot! Why didn't you ever tell me before this? Nick just mentioned to me this afternoon that you used to shoot targets when he was younger."

"I don't know, Maddy," replied Ma. "I guess I just felt like it was a part of me that had died, right along with your Pa. It takes gumption to be daring and different, and when your Pa died from the gangrene, my gumption went into the grave with him.

"But this land run has resurrected my gumption, and I'm willing to take it on for you two children and me. There may not be enough land to go around, but we're going to do everything in our power to make sure we're the most prepared settlers there, so we can get a piece of it for us."

Maddy looked at her Ma with a new sense of admiration. She appeared to be standing taller and straighter than Maddy had ever seen her stand, and the determined set of her chin let Maddy know that she was bound and determined to make this happen for them. All of a sudden, hope welled up in her. Maybe a new land wouldn't be so bad.

That night, as Maddy lay in bed staring up at the ceiling, the pink roses on the wall didn't seem quite as beautiful. She was starting to imagine the rolling grasslands of Indian Territory. What would it look like, she wondered.

And she couldn't get over the fact that Ma had learned to shoot a gun with Jesse James! Maddy could understand Ma's concern that other people didn't know about it. Everyone around these parts knew that Jesse had been bad news. He and his gang were rumored to have done some terrible things to folks, not just rob banks. The last thing Ma needed was for someone with a point to prove to try to force her to show how good of a shot she was. It would be dangerous for all of them if anyone knew.

CHAPTER 6

Practice

Saturday morning dawned cloudy, with a few flakes of snow falling. When Maddy got downstairs, she was surprised to see a huge mound of canvas stretched across Granny's quilting frame in the kitchen.

Granny's mouth was pinched around some pins, and she was stitching with her precise style onto the canvas.

"Granny, what are you making?" Maddy asked as she passed through the living room on her way to the kitchen.

Granny removed the pins from her pursed lips. "Since your ma is determined to make this fool run, we've got to make sure she is ready to go. This is the canvas cover for your wagon. I'm stitching in some pockets on the underside of it so that your ma can store things for the trip. It will also help her to be a little more organized with some of the things you'll need every day as you travel.

"Once I'm through with this, then Grandpa is going to treat it inside and out with linseed oil to make it waterproof. With the weather this time of year, you might hit some rain-storms, or even some leftover snow, before you get to Arkansas City, Kansas, where you'll be joining the other crazy fools."

The sheet of canvas seemed enormous. It was hard to believe they needed that much canvas to cover the hickory arches Nick had been working on. But she knew that Granny and Grandpa would be preparing only the best for them as they planned their journey. Even if they really didn't want them to leave Independence, Granny and Grandpa would never send them out without the proper supplies and protection.

Granny had left some biscuits and thick slices of bacon under a napkin on top of the stove. Maddy picked up a warm biscuit and three slices of bacon as she wrapped her cloak around her neck. She wanted to get outside and find Ma and Nick, to see what they were working on.

She found them with their heads huddled together in the barn. It looked as if they were trying to figure out something. Maddy hurried into the warm barn with its animal smells and the permeating scent of straw. It took a few minutes for Nick and Ma to notice her.

Ma looked up and smiled warmly. "Is there a particular reason you're out in the barn so early this morning, Maddy? Nick and I are working on calculating the supplies we'll need, and how many boxes we can fit into the wagon."

"Do you think you could show me how you can shoot?" Maddy blurted, her mouth full of the salty bacon. She wasn't interested in how many silly old boxes would fit in the wagon.

Ma gave her a smile and brushed some biscuit crumbs off Maddy's lips. "I can't do much here, because your Grandpa would wonder what in the world we were up to! A little bit later, we can saddle up and take a ride out to Grandpa's land, past the edge of town. Nick can do a little practicing, too."

After they were through figuring out how much the wagon would hold, Nick began to saddle the horses. Ma and Maddy went into the house to tell Grandpa and Granny that they were going to take an early ride before they started building the boxes for storing their things on the wagon. Grandpa gave them a puzzled nod. By the time they got back to the barn, Nick had almost finished saddling the horses.

"Here, Ma," he said, "You get on Ham, and Maddy and I'll ride double on Beans."

Maddy swung her leg over the back of the horse and wrapped her arms around Nick's waist. Ma mounted Ham, and they rode out of the stable yard.

Once they got out of town and onto Grandpa's pastureland, the three of them dismounted. Maddy watched in amazement as Ma pulled a pistol from the saddlebag. Nick had stuck half a dozen old cans in the saddlebag as well, so they would have something for target practice.

"Put the cans on those fence posts over there," said Ma "No one's anywhere near here, so we can have some fun."

Ma steadied her arm, took aim, and fired, not once or twice, but six straight times, and those six cans danced on the fence posts as the bullets hit.

"Ma, I can't believe this!" cried Maddy. "If only Clara could see you!"

"Maddy," Ma said sternly. "You *know* that Clara can't see this, don't you? Nor can you tell her about this. It *has* to be our secret. The last thing I need is someone hearing about me and deciding it would be fun to take me on in some kind of gunfight."

Nick looked at Ma in admiration. "Can I have a turn now?" he asked.

Nick had shot before and had gone hunting with Grandpa. But he was able to hit only one of the cans.

"We'll practice some more before we go, Nick," Ma told him. "We'll just make sure that Grandpa thinks that the practicing is for you, and I'll shoot a little. We just won't let him see how good I am with the gun."

After watching Ma and seeing how she could shoot with the best, Maddy's fears about their safety began to subside. Surely, they'd be just fine out in the wilderness with Ma and her rifle!

CHAPTER 7

Farewell

The morning of their departure dawned clear and cold. Granny's face showed tracks of tears. Grandpa was almost grim as he restrained his emotions. It was hard to imagine that the day they'd been working toward for so long was finally here. The wagon was carefully packed with supplies and food to last them not only until they made it to the starting point of the run but also until they had built their house of sod. They'd had to plan carefully to have a delicate balance between packing as lightly as possible, so they could run fast when the race started, and having enough supplies that they wouldn't starve.

As Granny busied herself in the kitchen, packing another round of biscuits into a pail with some smoked ham for sandwiches, Maddy stood at the entrance of the kitchen, taking in its warmth and inhaling the rich cooking smells. She suddenly realized that this might be the last time she would be in this room. It was a long way to Indian Territory, and even though Granny and Grandpa had promised to come visit them, it might never happen. Besides, they first had to somehow make it safely to the Territory and then actually make a claim on the land.

Maddy felt tears welling. It was hard to imagine the time when she'd considered staying behind with Granny and Grandpa. Now she was excited about their new beginning, but her heart hurt thinking about the farewell that awaited her. She'd already said goodbye to Clara the day before at school. The girls had promised one another to stay in touch with letters.

Instead of sharing her sad thoughts, Maddy bounded up behind Granny and wrapped her arms around her, saying, "I'm going to miss you so much, Granny."

Granny turned around and folded Maddy into her spry arms. She said nothing, just held onto her for what seemed an eternity. "May God be with you," she finally whispered into Maddy's ear. Then she pulled away and looked Maddy square in the eye. "This isn't a forever goodbye, Maddy. Before too long, your Grandpa and I will be traveling to the Territory to visit you. You'll be all right; I can feel it. So don't you be afraid of going today."

Maddy knew how hard it had been for Granny to say that. She couldn't trust herself to speak, so she only gave a nod, and then dashed outside to get another look at their wagon.

It was a magnificent thing, the canvas cover gleaming in the bright morning sunshine. Nick and Grandpa had replaced the large front wheels with smaller ones, so the wagon would be able to make sharper turns. Besides being sturdy enough to carry their loads, the wagon needed to be able to react quickly to Ma's hand as she drove it onto the unclaimed land where there were no roads to follow.

Going back inside to take her place at the breakfast table, Maddy could hardly swallow her bites of biscuit. Even Nick was uncharacteristically silent.

Ma looked at their faces and said, "Enough sadness, you all. This is a happy day. You'll see Granny and Grandpa again, I promise! Now we really do need to leave and get on the road. This first day will seem especially long to us, since we aren't used to traveling by wagon all day."

"The team's ready to go," said Grandpa. Their two horses, Star and Step, were strong, yet fast. Grandpa had purchased them at the finest livery stable in Independence the day after Ma had declared that they would be going to Indian Territory. The owner of the livery stable had assured Grandpa of Star and Step's speed and ability to pull the loaded wagon. Ma was still worried about the race, though. She wondered if they would be able to compete with the people that were alone on horseback.

"And I have one last thing to give you," said Grandpa. Nick and Maddy shared a look. What more could Grandpa have done? He and Granny had worked their fingers to the bone getting them ready for this move.

Grandpa went around back of the barn and led out a beautiful black quarter horse. Ma drew in her breath.

"It's for you to have for the day of the run," he said. "That day, even though you'll want to be together, you might not be able to move as fast as the folks that are alone on horseback. This way you can ride into Indian Territory together, but if the wagon falls behind, your ma will still be able to stay in the race. The horse's name is Betsy, but I've shortened it to Bet, because I'm betting on you getting a claim of that land!"

This time it was Ma who began to cry. This beautiful horse would take them that much closer to the realization of their dream. With a wagon outfitted for the race *and* a racehorse, they were in better shape than most of the settlers who'd be making the run.

"Thank you, John. You shouldn't have done this, but I'm glad you did." Ma gave her final hugs. "We'll send you a letter as soon as we can so you'll know how we're doing."

Everyone began to say their farewells. To Maddy it seemed as if the movements were in slow motion. She allowed herself to be folded into Granny's arms, lingering in her rosewater scent.

"You be good, child. You are going to write history. Remember that, and don't let fear take your dreams."

Ma looked at Maddy with a look of pride. She agreed, "You will write history, Maddy! We'll write it together." The solemn spell broke, and then everyone was moving outside to the wagon with its pristine white cover.

Grandpa helped Ma onto the wagon seat. "Maddy," Grandpa's gruff voice called her over. "Let me have a farewell hug, one that will last until I see you again."

Maddy ran to her grandfather and allowed herself to be lifted into his strong arms. She inhaled the smell of his hair pomade and told herself she'd never forget the feel of these strong protecting arms that had looked out for her since her Pa had died. Grandpa was a dear, and Maddy loved him so much. She knew Granny loved her too, but Granny was too practical to show it in the loving ways that Grandpa did when he brought her treats from the general store or took the time to patiently teach her how to ride a horse.

Grandpa saw the tears welling up in Maddy's eyes. "Now don't you go crying none," he said. "This is a happy time, the beginning of a bright future for the three of you. You'll find the perfect piece of land, and then Granny and I will be down in Indian Territory to see you."

"I love you, Grandpa," said Maddy, snuggling a little tighter into his neck.

With that, the tears welled in Grandpa's eyes. "I love you too, little Maddy. We will see one another again, so wipe those tears and let's say goodbye with smiles on our faces."

Maddy took a deep shuddering breath. The time for hugs was over. Ma motioned for Nick to mount Bet while Maddy clambered into the wagon.

"Farewell, and may God be with you, today, on your travels, and as you claim your land."

"I'm confident He will be. Goodbye!"

A chorus of goodbyes filled the air, and the travelers were off. Maddy kept swinging around from the front of the wagon to look back at Granny and Grandpa. The two figures grew smaller and smaller in the distance. Finally they were out of sight, and she turned her eyes forward, to what the coming days would bring.

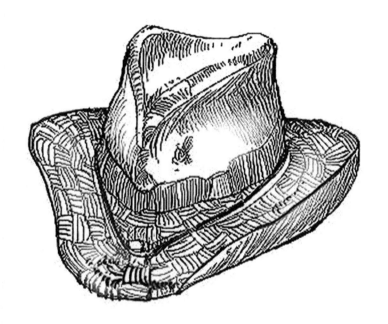

CHAPTER 8

A Visitor

T ime on the trail began to drag. After the first couple of days of excitement, Maddy quickly grew tired of the cold and seemingly endless landscape of hillsides. Ma had a trail map and appeared to know exactly where they were going, although once they left Independence, and then Kansas City, it was hard at times to tell the road from a well-worn cattle trail.

Maddy often preferred to walk; it could be chilly at this time of year, and the exercise helped keep her warm. Late spring snowstorms were still a possibility and Maddy hoped they wouldn't have to encounter one with a covered wagon as their only protection! Ma was wrapped from head to toe in her cloak, with a scarf around her neck to protect her from the wind. Nick had his hat down low on his head. Even though warm weather was around the corner, the winds seemed to howl endlessly across the prairie.

Maddy was already bored. She couldn't believe they were going to have to do this day in and day out for over 250 miles. As they battled the wind that was blowing fiercely across the Kansas plains, it was hard to envision the thrill of a land run.

After a stop for their noon meal, Nick put out their campfire, and Ma loaded the spider back on the wagon. The hot food had tasted good to Maddy, even though the beans and pork had been served with the last of the cold biscuits from Granny's house. As they were mounting the horse and climbing into the wagon, they heard a call.

"Hello!" It was a man's voice.

Nick jerked around abruptly on Bet. Even though they hadn't been alone on the trail for long, they'd already become accustomed to the stark emptiness of their surroundings.

Ma reached for the rifle and readied it to fire. Maddy's mind flashed back to the escaped bushwhackers. Ma set the rifle on her lap and, as they waited for the rider to approach, she nodded to Maddy that things would be fine. But Maddy could tell from the way Ma was sitting that she was nervous.

The horses waited for a command. Ma had the reins firmly in the grip of her left hand and the rifle in her right.

"Howdy, folks!"

By now the rider was close enough to observe.

"Greetings," called Ma, her voice neither friendly nor unfriendly.

Maddy used her scarf to hide her face as she took in the stranger. The man was tall, with scruffy whiskers. His worn hat rode low, covering his eyebrows. He pulled his horse up close to the wagon. Real close. Maddy felt a knot twist in her stomach as she breathed in his strong whiskey odor.

"Travelin' alone, ma'am?"

Ma avoided his question. "Is there some way we can help you?"

The man smiled, baring yellow teeth latticed like a jack-o-lantern. "Why, the question would be how kin I help you? You bein' all alone out here and all." He waved his arm as if to draw their attention to the vastness of the grassland and their solitude within it. There truly was no one in sight, no neighbor or another traveler to call.

Ma's jaw was set, "As you can see, sir, I'm not traveling alone. And if there isn't anything we can do for you, then we'll be on our way." She raised the reins, but Maddy noticed that her right hand didn't leave the rifle.

The man backed up a bit. "Now, ma'am, I have no reason to offend you. I just don't like to see a woman out all alone in the wild like this. My name is Albert Polk."

"If you'll excuse us, Mr. Polk, we'll be on our way."

Albert Polk gave a snort of laughter, "Mr. Polk? Most people call me Poker. Are you all traveling out West? Did you miss the last wagon train to come through here?"

"I don't see that where we are heading should be of any concern of yours, Mr. Polk."

"Poker!" he barked. Maddy shrank back as Albert Polk leaned nearer to Ma, "You've got a nice wagon here, ma'am." He ogled their wagon and team. "Maybe you need some help lookin' out for it, what with the fact you've only got a couple of young'uns with you."

Ma turned to Maddy. "Get inside the wagon," she said. Maddy cautiously began to sidle back into the interior of the neatly organized wagon. She saw a pair of scissors in one of the pockets Granny had sewn. She carefully pulled it down and hid it on her lap under her scarf.

"Where's your husband, ma'am? I can't imagine that he'd let someone as purty as you travel off all by yourself."

Ma set her jaw and gripped the rifle tighter. "It was nice to meet you, Mr. Polk. But now, if you'll excuse us, we'll be on our way."

Ma switched the team with the reins, and the horses began to move. Inside the wagon, Maddy gripped the scissors for security, not knowing what to expect. She could tell Ma was worried by the look of determination on her face. What would they do if Mr. Polk followed them? Maddy didn't have to wait long to find out.

Albert Polk pulled his horse up by Ma again. Nick blurted, "Ma!" but Ma just said, "Hush, Nick."

"Ma'am, I didn't get your name." The whiskey smell grew stronger again. Maddy peeked out and saw Mr. Polk trying to lean in close to Ma. He was by her right side, where her hand rested on the rifle. Ma pulled back on the reins, and the team stopped.

"Sir, we are leaving, and I'd appreciate it if you would take your leave of us now. We have no need of any company."

"Now that ain't a very friendly way to treat someone who only wants to help you." Mr. Polk pushed his hat back on his head, and Maddy peered out and got a good look at his black eyes. They were sunk into his face like little pieces of coal surrounded by fat flesh.

"Like I said, seein' as how you are alone, I'll just stay with you. You might need some protection. Plus, I imagine you've got some good grub packed away on this wagon," he gestured. "Why don't you just tell me where you are headed with this fine team of your'n?" Albert Polk again ogled the sturdy wagon and fine horses; then his pig-eyed gaze moved back to Ma.

When his gaze landed back on Ma, she turned to Maddy. "Come out here," Ma commanded, handing the reins to Maddy. "Hold these. Tight!" And an instant later, she had raised the rifle and aimed it at Albert Polk. "I've told you we don't need any help or you staying with us."

At the sight of the rifle, Poker pulled back on his leather reins. "I see." His eyes turned ugly. "You don't want to do this, ma'am. There's an awful lot of trail and not many people around here." He lowered his voice to a menacing whisper, "I wouldn't be threatenin' someone who's only trying to be friendly."

"Your kind of friendly we can do without. I suggest you let us be and do not follow us, or I'll be obliged to use this rifle."

"You can take your sorry horses and wagon and go! I'll leave now, but be warned: the next time our paths cross, I won't be so friendly." And with that, Poker wheeled his horse around. He gave a slap of his reins and rode his horse hard back across the prairie in the direction he'd come.

Only after he was out of sight did Maddy feel Ma's shoulders relax. Nick was worried. "Ma, do you think he'll be back?" he asked.

Maddy hoped he wouldn't. His whiskey breath and black pig-eyes had terrified her.

"It will be all right, children. I'm sure he won't be back." Turning, Ma noticed the scissors on the wagon seat. "Goodness, Maddy, why do you have the scissors?" Ma took in the fear still etched on Maddy's face. "Honey, people like him like to act big and brave to get what they want. I showed him to be the coward he is, so he won't likely come messing around us again. Let's put these back up in the pocket so they don't get lost. And to be on the safe side, let's get some miles between us and Mr. Polk. Come on, let's go. Don't let him spoil our adventure!" Ma signaled Star and Step to roll on out. Nick rode ahead every so often, scouting the road to make sure there was no one else around.

After about an hour, when they'd gone a distance without another sign of Poker, Maddy started to relax. Ma was right. Pig-eyed Poke wouldn't be back. But the encounter had given her a new uneasiness that didn't go away. Their vulnerability had suddenly become real. Even though Ma was a superb shot, Maddy realized how alone they really were on their journey.

After traveling a few more miles, they stopped to set up camp for the night. Maddy could tell that Ma was taking extra precautions.

"Nick, I don't think we need to keep a watch all night, but we do need to be careful. I want you and Maddy to sleep in the wagon. We're going to tie the horses to it, and I'm going to sleep underneath with the revolver ready. I wish we had a dog to help us listen for intruders, but if we have a plan on how we're going to get some rest, I think we'll be fine."

Nick soberly set about making their camp. He'd been frightened by Albert Polk too, and wanted to make sure they were safe.

Once they had made preparations for nightfall, Ma began heating up beans and pork over the campfire. She could read the concern on their faces that night as they sat around the campfire picking at their food.

"Children," she said, laying her spoon in the tin plate, "we've only just begun our journey, and we can't have someone like Albert Polk ruining it for us. I know we'd like to think that all the people we meet are good folks like us. Unfortunately, that isn't the way of the world. We need to be smart, but not fearful."

"But, Ma," cried Maddy, "what would we have done if he had insisted on staying with us?"

Ma looked at their grim faces. She smiled, "I think you know what we would have done. We have a plan in place, and you both need to have confidence in me. One old drunk like Albert Polk sure isn't going to scare me off. He wouldn't be able to draw his gun before I'd have his hair parted, clean as a whistle."

At that image, Maddy and Nick began to laugh. Ma was right; she was one of the best straight shooters around, so they really had no reason to fear.

"If anything, we'll need to be more fearful of the wildlife when we get off the Santa Fe Trail and head south out of Council Grove. Right now, this is pretty common traveling ground, and we'll probably see some folks coming and going. Once we do head south and follow the railway lines into Arkansas City, I don't know how many people we'll see on the road.

"I'm sorry we had to have that little scare today, but, if nothing else, it will help us remember that we need to be careful in our dealings with people and how we take care of ourselves camping at night." Ma looked at Maddy, "Darlin', don't trouble yourself grabbing something like those scissors if we have another encounter. Nick and I know how to shoot, and we have our guns. I'm afraid someone could use the scissors as a weapon against you, so leave the protecting to us, all right?"

Maddy nodded. Nick took the dirty pan and scraped it out with some clean river sand they had stored in a can, while Ma helped lift Maddy up into the wagon to settle into the bed. "You both get your rest," she said. "I'll be sleeping here under the wagon with this warm quilt wrapped around me. We'll head out early in the morning. We want to make it to the Big Blue River Ford by tomorrow evening and cross it before we settle for camp. To do that, we'll have to travel a good twenty miles tomorrow. That shouldn't be a problem, since we're traveling across the plains and have this good road."

"How far did we go today, Ma?" Nick asked.

"I'd say about thirteen miles. We're going to be pushing hard with our traveling, but as long as the weather is good, we need to cover as much ground as possible. We don't want to take a chance of having anything detain us. We have to be there in plenty of time to line up for the run."

Fellow Travelers

After about four more days of traveling, Maddy felt like screaming from boredom. As they packed up the wagon the morning after camping at High Water Creek, all she could think about was her life back in

Independence. She missed Granny and Grandpa. She missed Clara and her other friends at school. Goodness, she even missed Miss Busby! The novelty of traveling along the Santa Fe Trail was wearing thin. The wildlife along the roadside was no longer cute. The jackrabbits were annoying, the slithering snakes disgusting, and even their beautiful horses were starting to look tired. She wished desperately that she could escape this endless prairie with the wind howling like a pack of wolves.

Ma did her best to chatter, trying to relieve some of the boredom. She kept saying they needed to press on, talking about how nice the road was, and wondering how they would travel south to Arkansas City once they had to leave the Santa Fe Trail. She talked about what their new home would look like, describing the trees that grew in Indian Territory that had purple flowers on them in the spring. And Maddy could have sworn she pointed out every bird and butterfly they passed.

The dreariness of their travels was broken up when they met up with a small band of pioneers that were traveling to California. Maddy had to admit that having some company for a couple of days helped as they traveled along the trail. One of the families had a daughter her age, June Ann. It wasn't as good as having Clara with her, but June Ann was just as lonely for a friend as Maddy. While the adults took time to visit and take care of mundane tasks like washing clothes, Maddy and June Ann struck up a quick friendship.

Late one afternoon, Maddy and June Ann were playing at the edge of the creek while their mas were cooking supper. The girls had spotted some tadpoles and were trying to catch them in their hands. Needless to say, they weren't having any luck! Sitting back and giggling about how silly they looked, Maddy began to have the uneasy feeling that she was being watched. She shushed June Ann, and the girls sat listening.

A horse whinnied nearby. Turning toward the sound, Maddy glimpsed a man on horseback. He was riding away from them, and the way he was hunched over his horse made her think of Poker. June Ann looked at Maddy questioningly, but Maddy shrugged it off. No need to tell June Ann about what had happened to them on the trail. She didn't want to frighten her!

She meant to tell Ma about it, but when she and June Ann made it back to camp, Ma was visiting with June Ann's ma and smiling and laughing for the first time in days. She looked so relaxed that Maddy didn't want to cause her to worry, so she said nothing. After all, she hadn't been sure it was him. Their two families ate together that night, sharing their meals, and dreaming aloud about the new way of life that awaited them at the trail's end.

The following morning, they said their farewells to their new friends who were traveling on west, and Maddy felt a lump in her stomach. "Good luck in California, June Ann!" She didn't realize how much she'd enjoyed the company after all of the lonely days on the trail with only Nick and Ma to talk to. Not only had they enjoyed having folks to talk to, they'd felt safer being with the group. At least *she'd* felt safer. Once the band of pioneers left, Ma looked at Maddy and Nick. "Cheer up," she told them. "We'll meet nice folks again. I hope they have success in their new lives, just like we will!"

Maddy and Nick exchanged glances. Now that it was back to the three of them, it felt awfully lonely. Worried thoughts of Mr. Polk entered Maddy's head again. Also, she dreaded getting back in the wagon. She didn't know which was worse: walking beside the wagon, jumping over the cow patties that dotted the road, or riding in the wagon while her bones felt like they'd been beaten with the butter churn from the constant rocking.

"We're going to make it to Council Grove by around noon today," Ma tried to bolster their spirits. "They're supposed to have a good general store there, and maybe even a place where we can get something to eat that isn't trail food. How would you feel about that?"

Not eat salt pork and beans for lunch? Maddy looked over at Nick and felt a smile coming on.

"That sounds real good, doesn't it, Maddy?" Nick said.

Maddy nodded her head, "I'd love to have something different, Ma. Not that I haven't been fine with what we've had, but well, it's just…" Maddy's voice trailed off.

"It's not your Granny's hot biscuits with melted butter and honey oozing out of 'em, is it, darlin'?"

Maddy shook her head.

"Well, don't you worry. We'll have a chance to catch our breath in Council Grove. We'll spend the night there as well, and I'll talk to the folks to see about the best way to travel on down to Arkansas City."

C H A P T E R   1 0

Bur Oak Tree

Ma told Maddy and Nick that she thought they would have seen more travelers along the Santa Fe Trail, but she guessed they must have left Independence too early. The few folks they had passed seemed friendly enough, but for the most part were headed to Oregon or California. Most pioneers left Independence, Missouri, for the Oregon Trail in April in order to reach their destinations or cross the Rocky Mountains before snowfall. With the land run set for April 22, Ma had known they didn't have the luxury of waiting to travel with an official wagon train for part of the distance.

As they neared Council Grove, Maddy felt her spirits rising. Ma had said they could spend the night camped near town. Hopefully there would be a restaurant where they could eat something besides biscuits, beans, and salt pork!

Nick could hardly contain himself with the thought of a break in the ride. "Ma, can I ride on into town and check things out? Then I'll ride back here on Bet and let you know what I see."

"That's a fine idea, Nick. You go on!" Nick took off like a shot. Ma turned and gave Maddy a smile. "He needs to feel like a grown-up sometimes. And it will be good to know what the town is like."

The wagon rolled on the endless prairie. Finally Nick rode back into view. "Ma, there's a place to eat called the Hays House. They're supposed to have good food. There's also a tree in town, a big bur oak, that folks use as a post office. It has a hollow in it where you can leave messages. Then people willing to deliver the mail take the letters with them as they travel back and forth on the trail."

"Maybe we could write a letter to Granny and Grandpa," Maddy suggested.

"That's a wonderful idea! We can do that while we enjoy a meal at the Hays House."

Their time in town lifted their spirits. Maddy had some piping hot chicken and noodles. They weren't as good as Granny's, but tasted delectable after the weeks of trail food. While they ate, Ma wrote a letter to Granny and Grandpa in her flowery penmanship to let them know they were as far as Council Oak and still in good spirits.

"When do you reckon they'll get the letter?" asked Nick as they wedged the letter into the oak tree.

"No way of knowing, son. I guess when someone is headed back East, they'll take it with them. Now let's find us a place to camp near town."

Ma and Maddy hopped up onto the wagon seat while Nick mounted Bet. They had started down Main Street when they heard a familiar, "Hello!"

All three turned toward the saloon doorway in time to see Albert Polk waving at them.

"Imagine seeing your fine family again, ma'am!" he drawled, stepping off the wooden planked walk and approaching them in the street.

"Steady girls," said Ma to Star and Step. Then she turned to the man. "Mr. Polk," she said warily.

Albert Polk leered, showing his jack-o-lantern teeth. "So, where are you going, ma'am? I think I told you it weren't safe for a woman to be out travelin' on her own."

"As I said before, I don't believe where we are going is any of your concern."

Poker took a step closer to the wagon. "Let me tell you something. I've decided to make it my concern, ma'am. Seems like our paths keep crossing, so maybe that means I need to help your little family out." He looked over at Nick, who was scowling at him. Maddy shrank behind Ma's back.

"Mr. Polk, we are going now," Ma said, "and you need to take your leave of us or I'll have to go in and talk with the sheriff."

"Now, now, no need to go and get the sheriff involved here. I'll leave you be."

Albert Polk turned to walk away. Then he wheeled around and gave them one last look with his black pig-eyes. "For now," he said menacingly.

Maddy could feel Ma trembling under her cloak. But to look at her you'd never know she was upset. Ma just slapped the horses' backs with the reins and nodded for Nick to follow. They rode on out to the edge of town to set up camp.

"Ma, why didn't you just take care of Poker right then?" asked Maddy. "I don't like having to worry about him bothering us."

"I don't like how he's reappeared but I really don't think you have anything to worry about, darlin'. Like I said before, people like him that try to act so big are nothing more than cowards. He doesn't have the courage to really bother us. He just thinks we're an easy target since we don't have a man traveling with us. Let's go find us a place to camp for the night. I might even try to mend some of our clothes since we'll have some extra time here."

CHAPTER 11

A Shot Is Fired

Later that evening, after they'd enjoyed a quiet supper, Maddy was playing cards with Nick while Ma was mending the hem on one of Maddy's skirts. She'd caught it on her boot climbing up into the wagon. Maddy had learned she had to climb carefully into the wagon, using the wagon spoke as a step in order to get safely on top.

Suddenly, the family heard horse hooves. A shadowy figure emerged from the picket line. And a moment later, Albert Polk stepped abruptly into the light of their campfire. He didn't say a word, just loosely hooked the reins of his horse to their picket line and walked up to them.

Maddy could tell Ma was in a quandary. Her lap was covered with the dress and her pistol was tucked under the wagon cover.

"Listen up," Polk said. "I can tell that you plan to make that land run by what you're carryin' in this here wagon." He paused and grinned his yellow grin. "That's a mighty fine horse there." He motioned to Bet. "I might be obliged to take my leave of you if I could have yer horse. You might still be able to take a claim, with just yer wagon."

Ma glanced over at Nick. He read her eyes well. While Polk was looking at Ma, Nick quietly began making his way to where the rifle lay.

"Mr. Polk, you're right," Ma said, trying to keep his attention on her. "We are going to make that land run. And we're going to make it with our wagon and team, *and* with our quarter horse. I've told you before, and I tell you again. You'd best take your leave of us."

Nick had the rifle in his hand. But as he was turning back to the campfire, he stepped on a branch. At the snap of the branch, Polk whirled around, reaching for his pistol. In a flash, Maddy jumped up from the log she'd been sitting on, and lunged for Polk. She hit him head-on in the stomach and caused him to lose his balance. Poker fell on his backside landing near the campfire with Maddy on his belly punching him with her fists.

"Get out of the way, Maddy!" Nick yelled, raising his rifle.

Ma stood up and reached under the wagon cover for her pistol. "I've got him, Nick!"

Maddy scrambled to get out of the way as Polk rolled over from the edge of the fire with his gun raised at Nick. Ma aimed the pistol and shot. Polk screamed and grabbed his leg. Maddy stared at his jeans, watching the blood start to seep through the material. Ma ran close enough to kick his pistol out of his reach and nodded for Maddy to pick it up.

"Get out of here, now!" she yelled. "Get on your sorry horse and ride off and leave us. And if I see you again, I won't ask questions. And next time, I won't be aiming for a leg, Mr. Polk."

Polk hunched over his leg. He glared at Ma. "I'm leaving for now," he growled. "But I plan to make that run as well. You'd best be careful and not get in my way down in the Territory. The way I see it, there could be lots of trouble. Why, there's probably not even enough land to go around. No one would question a shooting if someone was to try to jump a claim." With a struggle, he managed to mount his horse, and rode out toward town.

As soon as he was gone, Ma began to shake. "Lands, children! In all of my days of shooting, that's the first time I ever had to shoot at a man. I'm sure he'll be fine—I only nicked his leg. But I'm afraid we've made an enemy. A dangerous enemy."

They slept restlessly that night. The next morning, Ma urged them to quickly pack up the camp and head on out. "The closer we get to Ark City, the more people I'm sure we'll see. I think we'll all feel better if we aren't traveling alone. Come children, let's not lose sight of our dream and why we are here!"

City of Tents

As they neared Cowley County, Kansas, where Arkansas City was located on the northern border of Indian Territory, they encountered more wagons. Maddy couldn't believe it when Ma had to fall into a line of wagons as if they were on a wagon train. People were walking as well. A well-worn road, defined by a pair of ruts that had a spring growth of grass in the center, had developed in the middle of the prairie.

Ma glanced over at Maddy and then nodded to Nick riding on Bet. "Some of these folks look as tired as I feel, and we haven't even made the run," she said.

Nick gestured to a rig off to the west that was coming to join the line of wagons. "Look at that, Ma," he said. Maddy craned her neck to see what Nick was talking about. The approaching wagon was packed to the top and appeared to be bursting at the seams with all sorts of furniture and children of every shape and size. A burly man drove his slow-moving team while a frail woman patted a baby's behind. Tiredness lined her face, and sadness was etched across her eyes. The older children had no smiles as they trudged along the wagon. Evidently, they'd had to walk the entire way on their trip.

"How will folks like them make it, Ma?" asked Nick. "There's no way they can get a good chance at getting a piece of land with that pathetic team and heavy wagon."

"I don't know, Nick," replied Ma. "I'm just thankful Grandpa got us Bet. I think she'll be our ticket to having a chance at some land."

Maddy turned around and faced the front again. She really didn't care about those folks or any others that they'd seen, if truth be known. She had grown sick and tired of being in the wagon. She was still worried about Albert Polk. And the thought of having to camp for the remainder of the days until the run began, then sleeping outside in a tent on a cold claim did not make her feel any better. Lately, she'd been wondering if she'd made the wrong choice. Maybe she should have stayed in Independence with Granny and Grandpa. She was daydreaming of her clean room with the rose wallpaper when she heard Ma exclaim, "Look!"

Maddy sat up straight. Unbelievably, Ma was pointing, something she'd always told Maddy not to do. In the distance Maddy could see something that looked like a low-lying cloud on the prairie. Squinting her eyes, she tried to make out what it was. "Ma, what are we seeing?" By now folks in other wagons were also pointing at the unusual sight.

"I think it's the tent city set up near Arkansas City. We're almost there, children!" Ma said excitedly.

Now Maddy strained to see. She wished the horses could move faster so she could get a better glimpse of this strange city made out of tents. The team, sensing their excitement, picked up their step just a bit.

"Will we be there soon, Ma?" asked Maddy.

"I think so, darlin'. The challenge will be in finding us a place to stay in the midst of all of those people. I plan to just use our wagon for shelter, not to set up our tent."

Nick said, "Ma, remember what Grandpa told us before we left Independence. He said to be careful of people trying to cheat folks out of their money and belongings once we got to Ark City. He said there'd be a lot of people who would be trying to take advantage of others, especially folks like us.

"Course, they don't know what we know. That you can take care of us and that you're smarter than any two-bit swindler."

Ma smiled at Nick. "We'll be just fine, son. I'm just ready to be there for a few days to check our supplies and rest a bit before we make the run. The horses could use a rest too."

As they neared Arkansas City, Maddy drank in the sight of the tent city. From the distance it appeared as if a flock of large white birds were hovering, moving ever so gently in the prairie breeze. As their wagon rolled nearer, she began to make out the different tents; slight differentiations in color set one tent apart from another. Maddy could almost feel the tiredness lift from the horses' hooves as if they could tell they were getting somewhere to rest.

"Ma, can I walk?" Maddy asked her mother, eager to get away from the rocking motion of the wagon. There had been times at night as they stopped for camp that she had trouble finding her land legs because they wanted to keep rocking like the wagon.

Ma looked down at Maddy, "Yes, Maddy, you may walk. Just stay close by the wagon. There are quite a few people around here, and I don't want you to be hurt by any of those wagons or their horses."

Maddy carefully jumped down off the wagon. Nick tipped his hat to her, and she waved back at him. Even though she was dreading wilderness living, just the simple fact that they were finished with the endless prairie quest for Arkansas City had raised her spirits!

About a mile from town, Ma pulled off to the side of the worn road and had Maddy get back up into the wagon. "I'm not sure what we'll encounter there," she said. "You need to be safely sitting by me. Nick, make sure you stay right with us until we figure out where we'll set up camp." Maddy clambered into the wagon while Ma checked the rifle to make sure it was loaded. "Nick, check your pistol, I want to make sure you have it loaded as well."

"Do you think there will be trouble?" asked Maddy with concern in her voice.

"I don't think so, but as a woman with two children planning on making this run alone, I want to be prepared for anything that might happen."

Maddy did feel safe with Ma by her side. She couldn't help but stare at the people and things as they rolled into the streets of Ark

City. She used the sides of her bonnet as a shield to hide her staring eyes.

Tents were set up along what appeared to be streets. At first it looked as if they had been placed helter-skelter, but it soon became apparent that there was some order in their arrangement. There were signs hanging on the tents or stuck on fence posts. "Ice for Sale," "Clean Water," "Horses for Sale," "Biscuits and Gravy—2 bits." Ma struggled to control the team as they made their way through the busy streets. Horses and riders were going in all directions; there were wagons ahead and behind, each traveler looking for a place to stop and rest.

"Here, ma'am, you can tie up your wagon over here!"

"Spots for wagons, over here, free bucket of water a day fer yer hosses!" Men were calling out to the passing riders and wagons, trying to get business.

Nick gave Ma a worried look. "How are we gonna know where to camp?"

Ma gave her head a little shake. "I'm not sure, but let's keep going. If we have to, we can go to the south edge of town and just camp on our own. I'd like to have a chance to talk to someone in charge and find out where the starting line actually is and if we can set up camp right near the line. Keep a lookout for a sheriff or marshal or someone with the cavalry."

Maddy was so taken by the sights around her that she gave up trying to be polite and not stare. Instead, her head turned faster than an ice cream crank. She'd never seen so many people on a street before; it was more crowded than Independence! And how they hollered at each other, trying to sell things! She was used to going into a quiet general store when Ma took her shopping back home.

Thankfully, Ma and Nick kept their heads. Nick spotted a cavalry officer dressed in his blue uniform. He pointed him out to Ma.

"Go, Nick," she said, "since you're on Bet. Go ask him about where we line up for the run. I'll pull the wagon over here, and we'll wait on you."

It didn't take Nick long to come back with a serious expression on his face. "What is it, Nick? What seems to be the problem?" Ma asked.

Nick's shoulders were slumped. "Ma, we've got to travel down through the Cherokee Outlet to get to the start of the line. The United States troops have to escort us through there. The good news is that the cavalry is going to start escorting groups down on April 18. The officer said we could join that wagon train of settlers."

Ma listened carefully and Maddy just sat there. Go further? She didn't know if her backside could take anymore riding in the wagon! "Ma, I'm so tired! Do we have to go any farther?" Maddy started to whine. She was so disappointed.

"Straighten up, Maddy. I thought, mistakenly, that Ark City was where the line started. Evidently we have to go farther south." Ma's shoulders drooped but it didn't take long for her to make a decision. "Nick, go ask that officer where we need to be and tell him our names and that we must travel with them. If we're with the army, they'll get us there, and we will have some traveling protection in case Albert Polk has managed to get on down here with his leg injury."

CHAPTER 13

Flooded!

The rain had been pounding all night on their covered wagon. The linseed oil had helped keep the moisture out but Maddy didn't know if it would hold much longer. They were getting a soaking! All three of them were chilly and miserable. Maddy couldn't believe they were going to have to pull out the next morning. The ground where they were camped was so wet and muddy it looked like pig slop. But because there were only four more days until the run, they had no choice. They'd have to drive the wagon in this mess to get to the starting line on time. Ma's face was grim as she helped Nick hitch up the horses. Then she finished checking their supplies while Nick saddled Bet. She wanted to make sure their belongings were secure. By the look on Ma's face, Maddy could tell she shouldn't whine about anything.

The weary travelers fell into line with their wagons and began the trek over the muddy roads and trails through the Cherokee Outlet. The excitement of seeing the tent city was long gone. The horses even sensed the change in spirit. They did their best to plod along through the mud, often straining to pull the wagon through the soggy prairie grasses. At times, the skies released more showers, but fortunately by noon the sun was starting to break through.

Maddy was silent, sitting by Ma on the wagon seat. She did have to admit that the land was beautiful. She could see copses of the trees with purple blossoms that Ma had told them about as they'd traveled across Kansas. The land itself wasn't just flat. It had rolling meadows, and you could easily tell where the rivers crossed by the thick forested areas near the riverbeds. The sunshine reflected off the rain-drenched grass, causing it to glisten like emeralds. Seeing the sun helped to lift their spirits a bit. Maddy began to hear folks in the other wagons talking, the sound of their voices drifting back to her on the soft southern breeze.

"Ho!" a loud voice called up ahead, and the wagon train stopped. Ma pulled back on the reins, and Star and Step slowed. Ma waited, leaning to the left to see if she could tell what was going on.

"Nick, ride on up and see what's happening," said Ma.

It wasn't long before he came back. "The Salt Fork of the Arkansas River is flooded from all the rain. They don't know how they can get us through."

Now Nick and Maddy turned to look at Ma. "What did the men say they'd do to get us across?" she asked Nick.

"They didn't say. The cavalry are all up at the front of the wagon train looking it over."

"What will we do, Ma, if we can't get through and get to the starting line?"

Maddy could hear the worry and fear in Nick's voice. Even though she'd daydreamed about Independence, she knew that Ma and Nick had put all their hopes on making this new claim of land. And, if the truth were told, Maddy wanted a claim as well. She was just ready to *be* there, living on the new land instead of sitting on the wagon for yet another day.

"Ride back up there, Nick. Don't leave until you find out what they have planned. We've got to get through today in order to make it to the starting line in time to make the run."

Nick rode off on Bet and Ma turned to Maddy, "It could be awhile before we hear something. Let's get off the wagon and make something to eat so we're ready to travel when they give us instructions."

By the time they had the food ready to eat, Nick was back with news. "They think they have a plan," he said, eyeing the hot beans and pork. Ma handed him a tin plate with the steaming mixture. Nick took a bite, wiped his mouth on his sleeve, and continued, "The river is so high there's no way it's going to go down in time for all of us to be able to get across and get to the starting line. But one of the officers found a Santa Fe Railway station downriver, and they're going to take boards from it and plank the railway bridge so wagons can cross."

"We're going to take our wagon and horses across a bridge made of planks?" Ma asked disbelievingly.

"They said that when we get to the river's edge, we'll unhitch our horses. We'll have to walk across, the three of us pulling the wagon. Then, once we're safely over, we'll go back to get the horses and lead them across."

All of a sudden, Maddy's dinner didn't set well. This plan sounded scary and dangerous!

Ma's lips were set in a straight line, and Maddy couldn't tell what she was thinking. Finally, Ma looked up at them and said, "Clean this up, children. Then we need to get to the water's edge to do this thing. We've come this far; we aren't going to allow a swollen river to turn us back."

By now, the cavalry had begun riding down the line of the wagons and were passing along the news. As Maddy helped clean up their dinner pot with the river sand and cover the fire with dirt, she looked at the folks in the wagons nearby. She could tell that some of them were arguing about what to do. However, Ma was resolute. She'd made up her mind, and they were going to cross that makeshift bridge.

One cavalryman was riding from the back of the line towards the river. Ma called out to him, "Sir, we want to make the crossing!"

He wheeled around on his horse and made his way over to Maddy, Ma, and Nick. "Are you sure, ma'am? Some folks are too fearful to try."

"We're not turning around and going back to Independence because of a flooded river. Tell us what you need us to do," Ma said firmly.

The cavalry officer looked at Ma admiringly. "You've got gumption, ma'am. Tell you what, pull out of the line and follow me."

Ma and Maddy climbed up onto the seat and Nick mounted Bet. Others around them watched as they pulled out of the wagon train and made their way to the edge of the river.

Once they got to the front of the wagon train, Ma reined in the horses, "Whoa!" she called to Star and Step. "Here, Maddy—hold onto the reins while I go look this over."

Maddy waited with the reins tight in her hand. She could tell the horses were nervous by the way they were shifting back and forth on their feet. Nick gave her a look. "Hold 'em tight, Maddy!" he shouted. "They're nervous about the water. They think they're going to have to walk through it."

Maddy didn't blame them for being nervous. The water boiled in the riverbed, and it was almost to the top of the bank. She didn't want to cross it either, much less on a makeshift bridge made of boards from some railway station!

The soldiers were finishing their work on the bridge. One young cavalryman who was watching the work said to Maddy, "This is what we do when we're on patrol. It will be safe. We're trained in making bridges when we enlist." Maddy was doubtful that it could be safe. But she'd have to do whatever Ma said.

CHAPTER 14

The Crossing

The soldiers were almost finished laying the planks and attaching them to the railway bridge. Ma walked back to the wagon. "This isn't going to be easy, children," she said. "We have to listen and be cautious, but we'll be fine. The cavalry knows what they are doing. The bridge will hold. We just have to be calm and keep the horses calm. That man over there is Mr. Smith. He said he would take his wagon across first. I told them we wanted to go next in line." Ma didn't say it out loud, but she wanted to cross the makeshift bridge early in case it didn't hold up for long. They *had* to make the start of the land run.

Maddy held her breath as she watched Mr. Smith unhitch his team of horses. A couple soldiers took the horses over to a picket line and tied them up. Then, since he was traveling alone, the two soldiers helped him pull his wagon to the makeshift bridge. Very slowly they began the walk across the planks. The planks didn't shift, and in a matter of a few minutes, Mr. Smith's wagon was safely across. The more difficult task was when he began walking back across the roiling river to retrieve his horses. Balancing and walking on the narrow bridge with no rails was difficult. Mr. Smith kept his arms out to steady himself. Once he stepped onto the ground on the north side, all the travelers clapped. He'd proven the bridge could hold.

"You go on, ma'am," he said to Ma. "I'll wait to take my horses across so you can get your wagon to the other side."

Maddy jumped off the wagon when Ma told her to. "Maddy, I think you'd be better off holding onto me as Nick and I pull the wagon. I want you to look straight at my side as we cross. Focus on getting across and do not look down! Once we get the wagon to the other side, I want you to stay there while Nick and I cross again to get the horses."

Maddy nodded. She was scared to death, afraid one of them would fall into the river and be washed away.

The family began their crossing, pulling on the tongue of the wagon. Maddy's stomach was churning like the river. Now she wished she hadn't eaten the beans and pork earlier. She was afraid she was going to lose her dinner into the river. Maddy was holding onto Ma's waist and walking right next to her. She didn't try to help pull the wagon. Ma said her job was to just hold on and keep her balance.

She glanced up at Nick. His profile was as grim as Ma's. Both of them were focused on walking very slowly across the wooden planks while pulling the wagon. Thankfully, Grandpa and Nick had done a good job building the wagon, and it rolled easily. Maddy gripped Ma's waist tightly. To keep from looking down, she counted the roses in the sprigged calico on the side of Ma's dress. As she was ciphering how many total petals would be on Ma's dress based on the number of actual roses, she heard Ma say, "We did it! Maddy, step carefully onto the bank!"

Maddy looked up and realized that they had crossed over to the other side. The soldiers who were on the far side helped pull the wagon on up the river bank and parked it safely out of the way. Ma sat down in a heap. "I think we need to let another wagon get across before we go back for the horses. I need to settle back down."

Maddy could feel Ma trembling as she nestled up against her. Ma had obviously been more frightened than she'd let on. Nick sat down as well. His face was pale, but he was grinning. "Well done, Maddy! We'll get the horses across and be on our way before you know it." Maddy could only nod. She dreaded watching Ma and Nick cross back over the river to get the horses, but it had to be done. While they rested, another wagon safely crossed to the other side.

"I'm ready to go back now," Ma said to one of the young soldiers as she stood up. "Nick and I need to go get our three horses. It will take us two trips across. Maddy will stay here with the wagon."

The soldiers waved to the others across the river to let them know that Ma and Nick were coming back. Maddy stood on the riverbank, frozen. As much as she hated holding onto Ma's waist and crossing the river, at least she'd been able to feel as if she was somehow holding Ma in place. Now all she could do was watch as Ma and Nick clasped hands, each holding one arm out for balance. They began the treacherous walk across the planks. The crowds on both sides of the bank watched silently while the woman and teenager crossed. At one point, Nick stumbled slightly, and everyone gasped. Maddy clutched her throat, but he regained his balance, and they made it to the other side.

The cavalrymen brought the three horses to the bank. Ma talked to one of the young men and nodded as if she was agreeing to something. Then Maddy realized what was happening. Ma was going to let the young officer bring Bet across so they wouldn't have to cross the planks again.

The horses were skittish. Ma and Nick were talking to them, using their calmest voices to encourage the horses to walk across. First came Nick with Step. He made it across without incident. Relieved as she was to have her brother with her, Maddy couldn't rest until Ma was on their side of the river. Ma had made it halfway across when Star suddenly threw her head back and whinnied. Ma held on tightly to the reins, determined not to lose their valuable horse in the river. As the crowd watched, Ma hauled the reins down so that she could talk right into Star's ear. Somehow she was able to make the horse hear her over the sounds of the rushing water. Star settled down, and she and Ma finally made it across.

Now Maddy could rest easier. But Ma was still tense. She knew that Bet was their true chance for a claim; they needed her speed. The young soldier began his walk across. Bet was wild-eyed, but the young man kept his grip on her reins and got her safely across. The three of them gave a cheer as the soldier came running up the riverbank with Bet. Ma impetuously gave the young soldier a hug; then, together, she and Nick hitched the horses to the wagon so they could move it to an area to camp for the night. It would take most of the day to get all the waiting travelers across the river. They would set up camp and make their way to the starting line the next day.

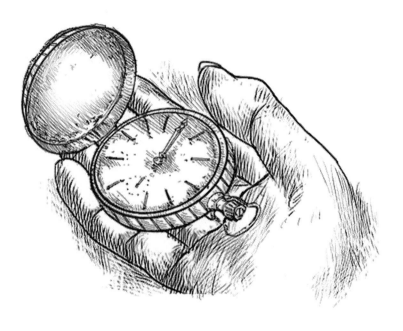

CHAPTER 15

Land Rush!

Maddy forced her eyes open. There was no more time for remembering how their travels had begun or for daydreaming about Granny and Grandpa's house. She looked up at the underside of the wagon. She'd memorized every board from the nights on the trail. According to Ma, they wouldn't have to sleep like this too much longer. Once they got their claim later today, and then got registered at the land office, they could start putting some kind of house together.

"Morning, Ma," Maddy said.

Ma was frying bacon over the small campfire. She smiled at Maddy. "Good morning to you, sleepyhead!" she teased. "Nick and I were wondering if you were going to sleep away the most important day of our lives!"

"I don't know how you can sleep late, Maddy!" Nick said. "This is the day we've been waiting for!"

"I didn't rest well last night thinking about the run," said Maddy. She rubbed her eyes and looked around at the wagons and horses. There were women and children, crying babies, and lots of men shouting back and forth. It didn't seem possible that by the end of the day all of these folks would have found new homes. Goodness, one of them might even get the claim next to theirs! As Maddy studied the faces of some of the settlers, she silently made mental note of who she thought might be a good neighbor as opposed to a pesky one.

"Maddy, come get something to eat. We need to get this pan put away." Maddy snapped out of her thoughts, rolled from under the wagon, and went over to the frying pan. Ma lifted four slices of bacon onto her plate and dropped two biscuits on top.

"Eat up. The run starts at noon, so we won't get to eat again until we've made our claim."

Maddy ate thoughtfully, holding one hand under the biscuit to catch the crumbs. "Ma, do you think there is enough land to go around for all of these folks?" she asked.

"I don't know, Maddy. There are two million acres, so you'd think they'd run out of people before they run out of land. We just have to make sure we have a plan and follow through."

"Ma, listen!" Nick called.

Maddy stopped chewing bacon to listen. Cavalrymen were riding among the groups of people, calling out instructions.

"Begin pulling into line," they called. "We need to get all folks onto the starting line as soon as possible to be ready for the noon start."

All of a sudden, the voices got louder. Shouts could be heard across the different camps as fathers rounded up their families and hurried them along. Those traveling alone quickly began throwing their bedrolls on the backs of their horses and mounting, to get to the starting line.

"Let's get going, children, hurry!" Ma said. She tossed the dirty pan into the back of the wagon, while Nick stamped out the fire.

Maddy quickly rolled up her quilt and blanket. Nick saddled Bet and then moved to harness Step and Star. All of a sudden, the weeks of preparation and miles of travel were coming together at noon on a beautifully sunny Monday, April 22, 1889.

Wagons and riders were already in line by the time they pulled into their place. The wagons and riders were lined up more than five deep in some places. Maddy looked around her, wide-eyed. How in the world were they ever going to get ahead of all of these people and make it to their claim?

She couldn't help staring at the mass of people and horses. Goodness, there was even a man on a bicycle! In the meantime, Ma and Nick were going over their strategy one more time.

"We want to head south of here towards the Guthrie township," Ma told him. "I've been looking at Grandpa's maps, and the piece of land I've got my eye on is not far from Guthrie, right on the Cimarron River. I'm not sure if things will be marked, but keep going due south till you hit the Cimarron. The river will be valuable to us. We won't have to rely on anyone for our water supply or worry about our wells going dry."

"Ma, are you sure you want to be the one on Bet? I could ride on down and stake the claim on my own."

Ma looked at Nick with a serious face, "No, Nick, you don't need the weight of finding the right place or dealing with armed men on your conscience. You know where we're headed. Just keep on course as the wagon falls behind. Once you hit the Cimarron River, you'll have to travel along its banks until you find me."

She turned to Maddy. "Maddy, I'm counting on you to be a lookout for your brother. He'll have to handle Star and Step very carefully to make sure we don't lose our wagon or one of them breaks a leg stepping into a hole. Your job will be to not only keep an eye out for me but also to let him know if wagons or riders are coming up."

"Yes, Ma," Maddy said soberly. "I understand." Then she could no longer hold it in: "What if we don't find you, Ma? What if that awful Albert Polk hurts you or takes our land?"

Ma reached her arms around Maddy. "Look at me, Maddy," she said. "We've got to have faith in our plan that things will work out. If Albert Polk rears his ugly head, it will be to pursue Bet and me. He wants Bet, and I'm sure he thinks he can grab our claim easily since I'm a woman. But I'm prepared to deal with him.

"And Maddy, even though I trust we'll all be together tonight around a campfire on our new claim, if something does happen to me, you have your brother to take care of you, and you know that Granny and Grandpa in Independence will do anything for you."

Maddy was silent. She had experienced every emotion since Grandpa had read that article in the *Kansas City Star.* From fear to excitement, dread to anticipation, she'd ridden a wagon full of feelings. But the hardest feeling to take on this day was the knowledge that she had no control over what would happen and that their dreams could be realized or dashed by day's end. Even worse, one of them might not make it.

"Sit tight, children! It's almost time." There was no more time for conversation. Ma was on Bet, her focus on hearing the starting shot. The horses could sense the tension. Several tried to pull out from the line. Wagons were rocking as folks settled in for the ride of their lives, and the horses strained at their bits.

The sun was bright overhead. Maddy squinted up. There were no clouds; the brilliant blue sky was totally clear. She couldn't see the open land in the Territory because of the wagon in front of them, but she knew from what Ma had explained to them that the cavalry was riding back and forth across the starting line to keep folks from trying to jump the gun.

Unexpectedly, a shot was fired! Maddy gripped the wagon seat.

"Not yet! Whoa, Bet!" Ma cried.

"What's going on?" "It's not noon yet." "Stay back! Someone is trying to cross the line!" There was confusion as people in the back of the lineup tried to determine what was going on. Finally someone from the front called back. "Someone tried to jump the gun. A soldier shot him dead." With that news the crowd grew quiet, the seriousness of what was to come washing over them. All the good-natured joking ended as folks focused on where they wanted to be and how fast they could push their team.

Ma pulled out her watch. "It's almost time, children. Just remember to follow our plan— and remember that I love you!"

"Oh, Ma, I love you, too!" cried Maddy.

"Me too, Ma," said Nick. "We'll be careful, and you be careful too!"

It was finally high noon. The shot rang out, and the wagons pulled forward. Some men were on foot; others were behind buggies or on bicycles. The race was on!

CHAPTER 16

"Yee-haw!"

As the wagon lurched forward, Maddy almost lost her balance.

"Hang on, Maddy!" Nick cried, "Hang on tight!"

The wagons raced forward, and to Maddy's horror, she saw a few people flying off their wagons as they tried to roll quickly over the uneven terrain. One wagon even tipped and rolled with its heavy load a few yards away from where they were. Maddy recognized it as the wagon they'd seen on the trail with the sad woman and baby. Thankfully, it looked as if the pa had been on the wagon alone. He was standing beside it shaking his head. There was no way he could get a claim now!

Suddenly the thrill of the race filled Maddy. "Go, Nick, go!" she cried. Nick glanced over at his sister and saw her eager face. Ma was off on Bet like a shot, Bet's long black mane flying as they raced.

"Yee-haw!" Nick yelled to Step and Star. It was almost as if the pair of horses could read their minds. They ran as fast as possible, avoiding every obstacle. Before long, Nick and Maddy were breaking ahead of some of the other settlers.

"Go, Nick, go! I can still see Ma up ahead!" Ma was ahead of them by over a hundred yards. Bet looked like she was soaring over the prairie.

Before long, Ma rode out of sight. Nick continued to push the team of horses. He drove them due south just as they had planned. The horses were running so fast that Nick didn't even have to raise the whip. Star and Step seemed to be spurred on by other horses that only had single riders.

As they raced over the prairie, Maddy looked back to see if they were keeping ahead of the main crowd. To her shock, she spied Albert Polk.

"Nick! I see Albert Polk! He's riding his horse and coming towards us."

Nick tried to lean over to see, but the wagon rocked back and forth over the rough prairie, and he gave up. "Keep an eye on him, Maddy, but hold onto the wagon. I don't want to lose you!" Maddy was bouncing like popcorn in her seat. She'd given up trying to keep her bonnet on her head; it had blown off and was on her back, held by the strings tied around her neck.

Maddy gripped the seat tightly and twisted to her right to try to see where Poker was. When she spotted him, he glared at her and shook his fist. "Nick, he shook his fist at me! He's riding hard, and I'm afraid he's getting closer!"

"Yee-haw!" shouted Nick to Step and Star. "Giddy-up girls! *Giddy-up!*"

"Hurry, Nick, hurry! I'm afraid of what he is going to do to us!"

Maddy turned again to look, fearful that Poker was catching them. "No!" she cried, startling Nick and the horses.

Nick did his best to control the horses, "Maddy, what is it? Talk to me! You have to be my eyes behind the wagon."

Maddy tried hard to catch her breath. "It was Poker, Nick. He was getting closer and closer to us. I think he was trying so hard to catch us that he wasn't paying any attention to anyone else. It was awful!"

"Maddy, *what* was awful? What in tarnation happened?" Nick glanced at Maddy.

"Another wagon came up beside him, and it looked like it startled his horse! I saw his horse rear back, and it threw him, Nick. He fell off!"

"Serves him right for trying to bother us. That will slow him down! If we're lucky, his horse will ride off, and he'll be on foot."

By now Maddy's chest was heaving. "But that's not all, Nick!"

Nick glanced over at his sister and could see the distress on her face. He turned back to the prairie in front of the wagon. "What is it, Maddy?" he shouted.

Maddy buried her face in one of her hands as if to bury the memory. "Nick, it looked like a wagon ran over him! I think he was run over!"

The horror of the sight, coupled with the fear of not finding Ma, was almost more than she could bear.

"Maddy, you don't know for a fact that he was run over. He's probably fine."

Maddy's chest was still heaving. "But what if he isn't, Nick?"

"If someone did run over him, they'd know it and take care of him. He isn't our worry."

"You think so, Nick?"

"I know so. Try to block this out of your mind. Instead, help me focus on finding Ma. I know we had a plan but there is a lot of land out here and lots of folks. I just hope we can find her!"

Maddy nodded, "I'll try, Nick. You're right. Maybe he didn't get run over. Everything happened so fast, and there are so many people out here!"

The horses were starting to tire. "I don't have the heart to keep pushing them; they've come so far," said Nick. "But we've got to find Ma."

Maddy turned to Nick, "We'll find her! Look over at that ridge. Let's go over there and give the horses a rest and see if we can find her."

CHAPTER 17

The Search

Nick and Maddy drove the team to the top of the ridge. They scanned the racing riders and wagons still making their way across the prairie. "I don't see any sign of her, do you, Maddy?"

Maddy shaded her eyes with her hands. "I only see men on those horses," she said. "We're going to have to keep going."

As they searched, they saw folks standing by their flags, showing that they had claimed a section of land. "What if there isn't anything left? What if Ma didn't get our land?" Maddy worried.

"We've got to believe that she made it. She and Bet looked like they were flying. We just need to keep searching." Time seemed to stand still as Maddy and Nick scanned the horizon for any sight of Ma. Step and Star were exhausted, but Nick had no choice but to keep looking.

After riding over rolling plains and past tree-lined creeks, Maddy started thinking she might not see Ma. They stopped several times, when they came to a hill or ridge, but there was no sign of Ma. "We've got to be getting near the Cimarron River," Nick said. "Peel your eyes for her, Maddy."

Maddy sat up as straight as a board. Finally she saw the river in the distance, but there was no sign of Ma yet. "Nick, I see some water. I think it might be the Cimarron, but I don't see Ma!"

"Keep looking. I hope she's there waiting on us! We may have to ride up and down the banks to find her."

As anxious as Maddy was, she wasn't prepared for the relief she felt when she spotted Ma and Bet a few hundred yards away standing with a flag in the ground. Ma had staked the claim! Nick urged the horses on to where Ma was waiting with a smile as wide as a mile on her face.

"Whoa, Step. Whoa, Star," Nick said as they pulled near. As soon as the horses slowed, Maddy jumped off the wagon and ran to Ma. "You did it, Ma. You did it! And the river is close, too!" The Cimarron River lay just to the south of the claim, its bank bordering their land.

"I thought I might not make it, but I just kept working with Bet, and she wouldn't let up. We rode hard, and somehow I kept passing other folks. I saw some cheaters whose horses weren't even lathered up, but I just kept going. I knew this piece of land would be for us."

"Now what do we do, Ma?" asked Nick.

"First thing, get the horses unhooked from the wagon and take them to the river to get a drink. We're going to set up a camp here, and we'll need to stay here tonight together to protect the claim. At first light I'll go into town to register at the land office."

That night it was hard for Nick, Maddy, and Ma to rest. There were folks roaming the land looking to see if there were any flags for claims that had been missed. Nick and Ma took turns keeping watch with the pistol. Fortunately, they didn't encounter any real problems. No one tried to jump their claim. Once people realized that it was taken, they moved on.

CHAPTER 18

Settlers

The next morning, Ma helped Nick feed the horses. Then they tied Star and Step loosely to a picket line. The horses ate the prairie grass and seemed happy not to get hitched to the wagon.

Ma saddled up Bet. "I'm going to the land office now to register our claim," she said. "I don't know how long it will take or when I'll be back. If for some reason you have trouble with anyone, including that sorry Albert Polk, don't be afraid to use the rifle. Leave it tipped against the wagon so you can get to it quickly if you need it." Maddy had told Ma about seeing Albert Polk trying to catch them during the land run and about seeing him fall.

"I hope no one will try to jump our claim, but you must be aware of what is going on. We're a few miles from town and I don't know where the closest lawmen are." Ma looked sternly at Nick, saying, "Take care of your sister." Then she gave Maddy her full attention. "You obey Nick and help him keep an eye on things."

"Yes, ma'am," they said.

As Ma rode off, Maddy worried again whether they'd be safe, but she knew better than to bother Nick. Instead, she set about helping him gather sticks. The longer sticks, Nick explained, could be used to make a lean-to they could drape the canvas over. The shorter sticks would be good for campfires.

Keeping busy helped the time to pass. They saw some people out riding on the prairie, but no one bothered them. Their flag was visible on the stake and their wagon showed that someone had already claimed the section of land.

It was almost suppertime before they heard Ma riding up. "Ma" cried Maddy, "did you get our claim?"

Ma triumphantly waved a piece of paper with writing on it. "Here it is, children! This land is ours!" She dismounted and ran to wrap her children in a bear hug. Nick and Maddy took turns looking at the deed to their claim. Seeing Ma's name and the President's signature on the paper was thrilling.

"You did it, Ma. You really did it!" exclaimed Nick.

"We did it together, children. This land may have my name on the deed, but it is for your future as much as mine. We'll build a life of our own here."

Ma paused. "Did you have any trouble?" she asked. Maddy and Nick shook their heads, telling Ma about the few people they'd seen wandering.

"Well, I heard lots of news in town." She continued, "It turns out about only one in four folks got a claim. There were close to fifty thousand people lined up around all the sides of the Unassigned Lands waiting to claim it! Even though we thought two million acres would be more than enough, it turns out that it wasn't. I'm just thankful Grandpa gave us Bet so I could race on ahead with her!"

"Were there many folks in town?" Nick asked.

"More than you can imagine! There were all sorts of stories about people and how they'd made their claim. One man even dressed like a woman so folks would stay out of his way. And the line at the claim office was so long. Some kids kept coming up and selling us water by the glass since we couldn't leave the line."

Maddy and Nick looked at one another in amazement! They couldn't imagine paying anyone for water.

"There was some bad news as well," Ma said. "There was talk about one man who was run over by a wagon. He was hurt so badly that the doctor in Guthrie couldn't do anything for him. According to the folks in line, the sheriff said he had a wounded leg and probably couldn't run fast enough to get out of the way of the racing wagons after he fell off his horse."

"Ma!" Maddy cried. "Do you think it was old Poker?"

Ma nodded, her face serious. "It was. Someone was able to identify him. He should have never tried to bother you children in the middle of the run. It was too dangerous! He was an adult and should have known better. I wouldn't wish that kind of end on any person's life, but he really chose the way his life ended. He lived dangerously, and he died dangerously." Ma took in their shocked faces. "Enough! Our worries with him are over. You two did nothing wrong yesterday. He put himself in danger."

"Are you sure, Ma?" asked Maddy. "I wondered if we should have stopped to help him."

"Maddy, you did the right thing to keep on going. You didn't know if he was hurt, and there's no telling what he might have tried to do, or what danger he would have put you and Nick in. You need to just try to put him out of your mind. We have too much to be thankful for. He made his choice to try to cheat and steal, and look where it got him."

CHAPTER 19

Plans

Ma leaned down so she could look into Maddy's worry-filled eyes. "We chose to follow our dreams the right way, and we made it. We don't have to keep wondering if we'll get our claim of land either. We did it. We're all going to write history in this beautiful territory. You, me, and Nick. I imagine it will be a state someday, and you two will get to say that you were here when it all began!

"Do you really think so? A state?" asked Maddy.

Ma nodded, "There were a lot of people talking about it in town today. They were saying that Indian Territory would surely become a state." Ma looked over and saw the pile of sticks that Maddy and Nick had been collecting. She turned to Nick, "Looks like you gathered some good strong sticks for our lean-to. We'll sleep in and under the wagon one more night and then tomorrow we can put the lean-to together."

Unable to contain her excitement, Ma suddenly jumped up and whirled around, flinging her arms out wide. "What do you think, children? Where should we put our house? It can be anywhere we want!"

Maddy captured Ma's excitement. "What about over here, Ma?" She ran over to the place she'd found earlier that day with the wild rose bush growing near a thicket of trees.

Ma followed, taking in the tall cottonwood trees amid a flat grassy area. "This would be a perfect place to build our house, Maddy," she agreed. "We could have it face south towards the river and put a window in the kitchen on the east side so we could see the sun come up every morning while we eat our breakfast."

Maddy could picture their house. She knew it would be small and that she wouldn't have her own bedroom, but that didn't matter. Better than having rose wallpaper to wake up to, she would have the beautiful prairie roses. And the real roses were hers to keep forever.

Nick went on to show Ma where he thought their barn should be situated and how many yards they should stake out for the corral. By the time they had talked and planned about where to put their buildings, the sun was low in the sky.

"Goodness, it's late," said Ma. "I don't know about you children, but I'm hungry! Let's get a fire started, Nick, so we can cook up our supper. Before long, children, I'll be able to order in a stove to cook on. We won't have to keep living like nomads. Think of it—hot apple pie!"

Maddy and Nick exchanged a smile. "Apple pie will be wonderful, Ma," said Nick. "I know we'll be ready for it."

"How soon can we have Granny and Grandpa come visit?" asked Maddy. "Do we have to wait until we get the stove?"

Ma smiled down at her. "Well, I have a little secret to share with you," she said. "Grandpa told me that if we managed to get a claim, he would come from Independence to build our house. He'll bring supplies as well, as much as his team can pull."

Maddy and Nick exchanged looks of happy surprise. "I actually telegraphed him when I'd finished at the land office today," Ma continued. "I suspect we'll soon be hearing from Granny and Grandpa on when they plan to leave."

Maddy started bouncing up and down on her toes at the thought of seeing her grandparents again. Her eyes shone. And they would have a new house to boot! Built by Grandpa!

"And," said Ma, "you'll get to start school before too long as well. There was lots of talk in town about getting the school built first thing and hiring a teacher. Just think about it,

Maddy. New friends! How does it feel to have everything so wonderful and new?"

With a heart full of joy, Maddy imagined what awaited her family. Now that they were here, safe and sound, it was hard to remember being in Independence and dreading the future.

The sun was beginning to melt into the horizon as Ma pulled the spider out of the wagon and started cooking salt pork, moving it around in the hot grease to get it crispy and brown the way they liked it. Nick began unloading more boxes out of the wagon to make room to bed down later that night.

Her heart full to the brim knowing the three of them had realized their dream, Maddy walked away from the campfire, down to the river's edge to watch the sun finish setting, a red ball going to sleep. She began dreaming new dreams; imagining all that the coming days would bring.

"Maddy! Supper is almost ready," called Ma. Maddy turned to run to the campfire.

"Sorry, Ma, I was just thinking about..." Maddy paused. "Well...about everything! When do you think Grandpa and Granny will be here? And *how* much longer until I can start school?"

"Soon, darlin', it will be soon," Ma smiled at her. "But you'd better sit down and let us have our supper now. You can start dreamin' again first thing tomorrow morning just as soon as the sun starts to rise over the Cimarron River."

The End

WORDS TO UNDERSTAND

Beau - a lady's boyfriend.

Bushwhacker - an outlaw who robs people, especially travelers.

Calico - a cotton fabric with patterns on it (often checked or floral).

Cavalry - members of the army who patrolled on horseback.

Cipher - to calculate math problems.

Pomade - a product used on hair that often had a strong perfume smell.

Influenza - the flu.

Land office - a place where records of land sales are recorded.

Linseed oil - an oil that would dry a yellowish color. It came from flaxseed.

Picket line - a line where horses could be tied to keep them in a close area while allowing them to graze on the grass.

Recitation - reading or reciting from memory a selected piece of written material.

Spider - a frying pan that had legs or feet attached to it so it could be set over an open fire to cook.

Town crier - A person whose job was to shout public announcements in the street.

AUTHOR'S NOTES

Did they have real races for land in Oklahoma?

Yes, the land run in *Cimarron Sunrise* was the first of several land rushes (runs) to open lands for settlement. People traveled from both the United States and other countries to race for the free land.

Could Jesse James have been Ma's friend?

It is possible Ma could have been a neighbor of Jesse James. I wanted Maddy's family to start their journey in Independence, Missouri, where most people began their journey to Oregon and California. I thought it would make the story of Ma being a sharpshooter more believable if the famous outlaw Jesse James taught her how to shoot. Jesse James was raised near Independence in Clay County, Missouri. His father was a Baptist minister and hemp farmer, his stepfather a doctor. Even though *Cimarron Sunrise* is based on some true events, the characters and their experiences are works of fiction.

Did people really leave mail in the tree at Council Oak?

The Council Oak tree was used for messages for travelers going east or west on the Santa Fe Trail. The messages left were typically related to information about traveling, such as where there were floods or roads washed out. The tree was used for about 20 years, but it was not used for mail in 1889 when Maddy and her family would have traveled through Council Oak. I thought it interesting that a tree could be used for a post office so I wrote into *Cimarron Sunrise*.

Did they have restaurants in the late 1800s?

Most of the time travelers had to prepare and cook their meals outdoors just like Maddy and her family. However, there were restaurants that were open for both travelers and the people that would live in a town. The Hays

House where Maddy and her family stop to eat was an actual restaurant operating in Council Grove, Kansas, in 1889.

Were there bad men like Albert Polk who robbed families?

Unfortunately there were outlaws and bushwhackers who tried to take advantage of others during the pioneer times. People had to be concerned about their safety as they traveled just like today.

Why was there a tent city?

In places where settlements sprung up so quickly, it was common to see tents staked first and then buildings were put up as soon as possible.

Could women have a claim of land on their own?

Yes, the Homestead Act said that women who were over the age of twenty-one and that were the head of a household could claim a 160-acre homestead.

How big is 160 acres?

If you were to take a square mile in your town and divide it into four equal parts you would have 160 acres.

Is it true that settlers had to cross the flooded Salt Fork?

Yes, the cavalry did escort a group of settlers that encountered the flooded Salt Fork. The cavalry officers tore apart a railroad station and used the boards to plank a railroad bridge.

Did anyone get shot at the start of the 1889 Land Run?

There wasn't a rider shot at the start of the Land Run of 1889. However, an individual (John R. Hill) was shot for trying to start early during the Cherokee Strip Land Run in 1893.

ABOUT THE AUTHOR

 A National Board Certified Teacher, Brenda works diligently to improve the skills of her fourth grade class while contributing to their personal development. Writing allows Brenda to communicate knowledge in creative ways. She has two adult daughters and lives in Tulsa, Oklahoma, with her husband.

Contact Brenda at
brendaturnerbooks.com

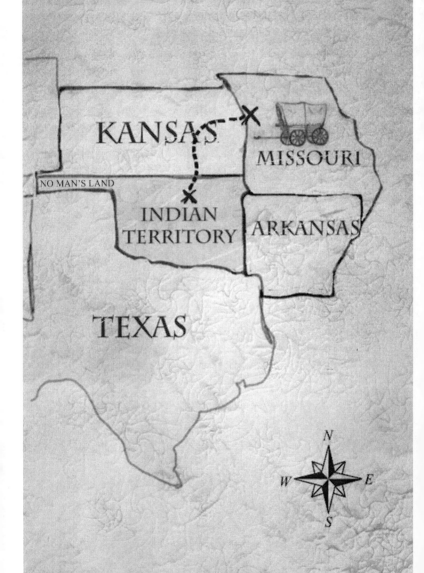